SUICIDE
— KING —

Jake Samson Mysteries by Shelley Singer:

SAMSON'S DEAL
FREE DRAW
FULL HOUSE
SPIT IN THE OCEAN
SUICIDE KING

SUICIDE KING

A Jake Samson Mystery

SHELLEY SINGER

St. Martin's Press • New York

Library of Congress Cataloging-in-Publication Data

Singer, Shelley.
    Suicide king : a Jake Samson mystery / Shelley Singer.
        p.   cm.
    ISBN 0-312-02293-X
    I. Title.
    PS3569.I565S86 1988   88-18845
    813'.54—dc 19   CIP

First Edition

10   9   8   7   6   5   4   3   2   1

for Adam

The author is very grateful to the following people for their help: Jean Askham, Voters Service Chair, League of Women Voters of California; Kevin Braaten-Moen, Political Reform Consultant, California Fair Political Practices Commission; Oliver Cox, Staff Counsel, California Secretary of State's Office; Emmie Hill, Registrar of Voters, Alameda County.

SUICIDE KING

—1—

I knew from the beginning that I never should have gotten involved in politics.

But I went ahead anyway. I listened to a speech about saving the world and I opened my skinny wallet and my big ears and stuck around to hear more. And that was why I was standing in a backyard in North Berkeley looking at a gubernatorial candidate swinging naked from the limb of a feather-leafed acacia tree. Not like a monkey; like a corpse.

It had been about fifteen minutes since my friend Pamela had called me with the news.

"Jake! Thank God you're there."

"Pam?"

"Come to my house. Joe's dead. Please. You've got to come."

"Dead?" A heart attack? Joe Richmond was a young man, in his forties, but . . .

She began to cry. "Hanging . . . from . . . a . . . tree."

"Oh, shit, Pam. I'll be right there."

I ran for my Chevy and drove much too fast down Telegraph Avenue, zigzagging around the UC campus and coming out on the side of Berkeley that's as far from Oakland as it can get.

I didn't have to search too hard for the place. The last time I'd been there was the night before. The house was a big two-story, Spanish-style set well back on a smooth lawn, shaded by a huge old avocado. Not the right tree, though. No one was hanging from it. I saw no sign of anyone living, either. I pushed my way through a side gate, following the brick walk to the back.

Pam must have heard the gate, or maybe my car pulling up, because she ran to meet me, grabbed my arm, and tugged me into the sheltered green privacy of the backyard, past the hot tub, until I could see it.

Hanging from a low branch, his bare feet just a foot or so off the ground, was the Vivo Party's favorite candidate for governor of California. He was wearing a thick hemp noose. On the patio bricks nearby, kicked over on its side, lay a small redwood garden bench. Richmond looked very dead, but I dragged the bench over, climbed onto it, and lifted his eyelid. The pupils were asymmetrical, the lids flabby, the glaze of death like a cloud. I touched his shoulder. It was cold. I stepped to the ground.

Pam was babbling.

"I should have cut him down. I know that. What if he was alive when I got here? But I couldn't do it. He looked dead. I'm sure he was dead. Jake, what if he was still alive?"

"I doubt it, Pam." I heard a car door slam out on the street. "Maybe that's the cops."

She got quiet, her eyes shifting away from me. "I haven't called them."

"Call them now."

She did.

I didn't cut him down, either. He wouldn't have known the difference, and the cops might as well get a crack at what was left of the scene. Pam had probably littered the yard with evidence of her own presence, and had called me—and was now calling the police—from a phone in the house. And then I had come marching in, moving the yard furniture and fiddling with the corpse.

I stood and looked at Joe Richmond. His handsome face was grotesque now, blood-filled, his head twisted to the side, his tongue sticking out. I was glad he hadn't messed himself when he died. I understood why Pam hadn't been able to bring herself to call the police. It was bad enough that two people who liked him were seeing him this way. If Joe Richmond had a flaw, it was personal vanity, pride in his near-perfect flesh. He should have been reduced to ash in a fire or lost at sea. He didn't deserve to die ugly because he'd hanged himself.

As quickly as that thought came, it brought one of those moments of certainty that go beyond reasoning.

I knew he couldn't have done it.

—2—

I didn't know Pam yet, back when all this began. It was another woman who got me into it in the first place. My friend. My tenant. My sometime business partner—if you can call unlicensed investigation a business—Rosie Vicente.

Rosie lives in the other cottage at my two-cottage place. We share the garden, the garbage can, the water supply, and the birdhouse-shaped mailbox up at the front gate. Sometimes, when I'm sorting out my mail, I can't help but notice some of hers. And one thing I'd never noticed a lot was political stuff.

As far as I knew, Rosie hadn't been involved in politics since she was a very young woman in the early seventies, passionately fighting for the feminist cause. She didn't fight much anymore, because, she said, she got tired of hearing different people say the same old things as if they were newly invented. But she was still a passionate feminist. After all, she said, what else could a female carpenter be?

Sure, she voted, because like me, she keeps hoping. We think pretty much the same things are bad, good, or funny. But she's just not into groups much.

So I was mildly surprised when I started seeing envelopes from the Vivo Party in her mail. And mildly annoyed when she invited me to go hear a speech by a man who wanted to be the party's gubernatorial candidate.

"Oh, come on, Rosie," I said. "You know how I feel about politics."

"Yes," she said. "I know. Politics is a trivial pile of shit, a ball game played for power and money. Fun and profitable if you understand the game, futile and frustrating if you don't. Right?"

"Right," I grumped. "Exactly."

"This is different."

"Oh, sure. They're the ones who want to save the planet, isn't that so?" She nodded patiently. "Like the Greens and Greenpeace and Earth First! and all those people?" She nodded again, a mother tolerating an adolescent son. "Well, they sound good. But I'm reserving judgment. Maybe they've got a secret agenda. Maybe they're tied up with too many other causes to be effective, too many knee-jerk pals bending them around and deflecting them. How can I trust anything that calls itself a political party? Why would I support someone who wants power and God knows what else? Why—"

"Oh, shut up," Rosie said, laughing. "I already know you think the only thing better than anarchy would be for you to be king."

"That's chieftain, not king. And actually, I've been thinking about that. Even Reagan aged in office. Maybe my hair would fall out. You never can tell."

"I think you should come."

"Oh, all right." So I went.

The speech was in a church in South Berkeley, just over the Oakland border and about a mile from my house. I drove.

"Is this guy we're going to see the front-runner?" She said yes, he seemed to be. "Okay, then, if this group is so terrific, so free of conventional political ties and all that horseshit, why isn't their front-runner a woman?" I turned onto Shattuck Avenue, a triumphant flourish of a right turn. Let her answer that.

"Maybe they want a candidate, not a burnt offering," she retorted. "Besides, there's a woman running close behind."

"Always a bridesmaid, never a bride. The woman behind the man, eighties' style. Seems to me that's hardly worth all the trouble she's going to. She is going to some trouble, isn't she?"

"Do you expect an argument?"

No, I didn't. A dozen other cars were cruising around the church, which didn't have a parking lot of its own. I slipped my '53 Chevy Bel Air into a spot about a block away.

The scene inside the church was familiar. A large basement room, the kind where neighborhood crime-watch groups sit and listen earnestly to representatives of the police force telling them how to lock their windows. There were the inevitable sign-up tables at the back, with intense young people handing out literature. I accepted a flyer from one of them. Rosie nodded to several acquaintances. I saw a couple of people I've run into around Berkeley and North Oakland, including a man who had, the last time I'd seen him, been involved in building an ark to escape the great flood. I guessed he'd been disappointed when it hadn't arrived on schedule and destroyed the world, and had gone looking for solutions to the world's problems, instead.

I glanced through the flyer. The main message was that Joe Richmond, the guy who was going to be speaking that night, was the strongest choice in a field of Vivos competing for the group's support as candidates for governor. That he was the candidate they should "vote for at the June convention." I found this puzzling. I didn't know much about these things, but I was pretty sure the gubernatorial candidates in California were chosen by primary, and that the primaries were also two months off, in June. But Rosie was yanking at my arm, so I decided not to worry about it and let her drag me along.

With ten minutes to go before speech time, the place was filling up fast. A news team from the Oakland TV station arrived, looking bored, then three more from San Francisco, looking even more bored. I figured they were disappointed no one was demonstrating outside, maybe carrying signs that said things like NUCLEAR WASTE CREATES JOBS and FREE THE PETROCHEMICAL SEVEN.

We managed to grab a couple of chairs in the back row. A quick count told me there were about 300 seats, filled, and by the time I turned around to check the standing room at the back of the house, it was filling up, too.

When I'd gotten a general fix on the audience, which looked pretty normal on the whole and, in some cases, even excited and happy to be there instead of just sincere, I turned back to the stage. Just in time to see a young man in tight-ankle jeans, corduroy jacket and narrow tie trot up the stairs and bound to the dais. He had graduate student written all over him, from his short, dark, curly hair to his white running shoes.

There was applause. The young man, with what was either charming self-effacement or incredible arrogance, did not introduce himself, but instantly launched into an introduction of the main speaker, a "man of business" from the Midwest who had started out in state politics there and had become aware of the "need for a new vision of reality, a transformation of values." After said business had moved him to Los Angeles—they were making a big point of this business stuff, maybe to confuse conservative voters?—he had gotten involved in the beginning of the Green Party's movement in the U.S. and had then become an organizer when the Vivos split off from the Greens to form their own party. I had only a vague idea of what that might mean. I'd seen a few news stories on the Greens, mostly about the German ones. I'd gathered they were a pretty recent phenomenon. As for the Vivos, I'd seen maybe one or two mentions in the press and only in the past year.

That was pretty much it for the introduction, except for, "Here he is, the next governor of California, Joe Richmond!"

Which caused quite a stir. As a man trotted up to shake the graduate student's hand and wave at the crowd, nearly everyone jumped up and cheered, at the same time doing a kind of two-handed salute, a double *V* for victory or V for peace, depending on which piece of history you were living. Maybe now it was a *V* for Vivo. Odd name, Vivo. Sounded kind of

Spanish, I decided. I made a mental note to ask Rosie where it had come from.

I say nearly everyone jumped up and cheered and waved their arms, because quite a few people, including me, just applauded politely. I guessed the less enthusiastic supported other candidates for the nomination. As for me, I hadn't heard anything worth cheering for yet.

But I was impressed. Standing up there at the dais, grinning and holding his hands in the air palms out—a gesture that seemed to combine "There, there now, I'm just a man," and "Hey, everybody, we're gonna win this sucker"—was one of the most astonishingly handsome and charismatic people I've ever seen.

I remember thinking that these folks had found themselves a Kennedy.

He was tall, which is always a good thing, especially if you're running for office. His hair was yellow as sunlight, shading to gray just above his ears. His eyes were bright sky blue with just enough wrinkles around them to imply good humor and wisdom. His teeth were, of course, perfect. His suit was gray and expensive.

Star quality.

Back in the sixties in Chicago, I went to see Judy Garland perform at a huge auditorium. Her voice was going by then, and I guess her spirit was faltering somewhere inside—this was not long before her death—but oh, my God, what that woman could do with an audience. We were all cupped in her hands through the whole show, intimately, passionately. The power of her presence was not something you see that many times in life. I was seeing it in Joe Richmond.

Star quality, magic, whatever you want to call it. The fact is, some people are smaller than their own bodies, some people fit their own space just fine, and a very few are much, much larger than life. They manage to fill a room all by themselves, and here's the real magic: they don't crowd anyone else out because they absorb everything around them. Joe Richmond was standing in front of us, filling the room, and holding everyone there comfortably inside himself.

The crowd had quieted.

"Whether or not I'm the next governor," he said, "I'm going to be very proud to be your first candidate."

The crowd went wild again. He smiled and raised his hands in that double-*V* salute, and stirred them up even more. Then he got serious, lowered his hands halfway and made quieting motions, a gentle pushing that said clearly, "I'd like to speak now." The crowd hushed and he began.

His voice was good, but not as perfect as the rest of him. It could have been deeper. It could have been a little less nasal. But it did have one important thing going for it. He spoke midwestern standard English, the kind that knows no accent. The kind that most Californians speak and that television actors and anchors strive for. Classless but classy.

His blue eyes blazed with a vision of glory as he spoke of a worldwide movement, of the need to preserve the integrity of the planet, of our symbiotic relationship with all forms of life. Of the duty to protect and to bring about ecological renewal. He used the words wisdom, care, respect and responsibility. He talked about peace, too, and he lost me because I don't believe it's possible within a single human, let alone among us all. But he caught me and dragged me back again by advocating decentralized political authority—I personally happen to think people can't govern themselves in units bigger than villages. And he held me when he talked about ecologically based economies and technologies.

All that stuff sounded good, partly because the man used none of the standard rhetoric of the standard left. Not once, for example, did he use the word *struggle*. But the hysterical cheering of the crowd made me nervous. There was something sexual about it.

Richmond concluded with a rousing call to the "defense and regeneration of life, a future of love and cooperation among the communities of humanity, living in harmony with all of nature, and an unswerving effort to deliver intact to the future the air, the land, the seas, the plants, the animals, the earth itself—our home!"

The crowd was on its feet, screaming, yelling "Vivo!" and "Joe! Joe! Joe!" Rosie and I stood, too. The TV people and several predators I guessed were print-media reporters rushed up front, mikes and pencils waving.

I was thinking, yeah, I'd give both my legs to see it happen, but I'd never have to make that sacrifice. Humans have been shitting in their own cave too long. Joe Richmond's vision was science fiction. We lived in a world where people thought birds were dirty and pesticides were clean. It made me want to cry, way down in some childlike core, but I was pretty sure that when I died, the earth would be a more poisonous place than it was when I was born.

"Jake? My God, you look so depressed." It was Rosie, snapping me out of my polluted blue revery.

"No I don't," I said. "What is this Vivo, anyway? What's it stand for?"

"It's Esperanto for 'life.'"

"Terrific," I said. But I let her talk me into signing up for their mailing list.

— *3* —

A little over a month later, in May, Joe Richmond came into town again for one last Bay Area bash before the June convention.

I'd been getting mail from the Vivos all that time, announcements, schedules, pep talks, and I'd read just enough of it to figure out why they hadn't run their candidates in the primaries. They couldn't do it because they weren't a legal political party. They'd tried to qualify with a petition campaign, but they hadn't gotten the numbers they needed. They said they got a late start. So what they were doing instead was having a kind of nominating convention where they would vote to support one candidate who would run as an independent. The candidates had agreed to abide by the convention's choice. As far as I was concerned, this was a pretty loopy approach to the electoral process. I lost interest and stopped reading the stuff they sent me, and I certainly didn't go to any of their meetings. So it was news to me when Rosie said there was going to be a benefit in San Francisco on the tenth of the month.

"Want to ride over with me?" she asked.

"I don't know. Tell me more."

"Great party, great entertainment, great cause, and an inside view of a Pacific Heights mansion. What more do you need?"

"The price."

"Hundred."

"Hundred?"

"I'll take you for your birthday."

"My birthday's in February, and I'd rather you gave me a date with Debra Winger. Really great entertainment?"

She named a famous impressionist and a sixties rock star I'd liked back then. "And some local acts, too. Joe Richmond will be in town for it, and Rebecca Gelber will probably come. I've never met her."

I'd been reading about Rebecca Gelber, from time to time, in my morning scan of the paper. She lived in the area somewhere. She was the woman who was running against Richmond for the Vivo endorsement.

I don't know what made me decide to go to the benefit. Fascination with a man who would be king? The impressionist? The rock star? The mansion? Maybe I felt guilty for making the Vivos waste all that postage on me. I agreed to go.

The benefit was still a few days away when Richmond hit Northern California and began to get more local press again. He was all over the place—Silicon Valley talking about polluted groundwater, San Francisco talking about the Bay, Sonoma County talking about the Russian River and sewage problems. I saw him being interviewed on the six o'clock news, and I read about him in the papers. Gelber was also making the rounds. She was, after all, the native daughter, and her people didn't take the opposition's invasion lying down. She was everywhere, too.

I was determined to have a good time, since I was paying so much for it, so on the big night I whipped myself into a party mood while I was getting dressed. I sang, I danced, I smiled at myself in the mirror. My twin tiger cats, Tigris and Euphrates, watched me from the bed with half-closed eyes. I ran a comb through my hair—it's blond and doesn't show the gray much, women like the curls, and it's hardly thinning at all yet—one last time, dumped some food in the always-empty cat dishes, and headed up to Rosie's.

"So," I said, as we cut down Fifty-first Street to the freeway on-ramp, "how come you aren't bringing a date?" We hadn't talked much lately.

"Between engagements," she said. I knew the social worker was long gone, but I'd thought the chef, Lissa, would be around for a while. I said I was sorry to hear it. "And you? Why isn't Lee coming tonight?"

"I haven't talked to her for a week," I said. "She's been on one of her work binges." Lee was an attorney who lived up in Petaluma. I'd been seeing her off and on for several months. Rosie murmured something consoling about that. We were crossing the Bay Bridge. It was a nice evening, with the fog beginning to drift in through the Golden Gate and lap up the western edge of the city. The City. San Francisco. All the other cities in the Bay Area are called by name. They are not The City.

When you take the Bay Bridge into San Francisco you ride the upper level and you get the full impact of the view. Riding back to the East Bay on the lower deck, you don't see much of anything. Which says a lot about attitudes around here. But what the hell, man, the East Bay's tough; we don't go for that fancy stuff anyway.

Pacific Heights, on the other hand, goes for the fancy stuff in a big way. This is the kind of neighborhood where mayors live, and internationally notorious attorneys, and society remnants of an older San Francisco where coming-out parties really meant something. The houses are mansions made of stone, like rocky crags looking down on one of God's most favored places.

The one we were going to looked like it had fifty rooms. Unfortunately, it did not have fifty garages, so my Chevy and I were on our own. I found a spot on the street, only three blocks away, and we walked back. Just walking on that street made me feel like I had money.

A butler in tails opened the door. He was very big and very muscular. He glanced at our tickets, and as he led us through the reception hall I whispered to Rosie, "He looks like a bouncer." She favored me with an exasperated smile.

The butler-bouncer escorted us to a double sliding door, at which stood a large blond woman who also could have been a bouncer. She wasn't wearing a horned helmet, but I could imagine one. Her pale hair was captured in a braid that circled the top of her head, and when Rosie handed her our tickets, she smiled and said, "Ja, danke, Rosie."

"You're welcome, Gerda," Rosie replied.

The room we entered was huge, maybe seventy feet square. What kind of house, I wondered, had a living room that size? Then I realized the "living room," or parlor, or whatever this place had, was somewhere else on the first floor. This was a ballroom. It was furnished with a lot of folding chairs, some—get this— sconces on the walls, a couple of banquettes between three large draped windows, a big refreshment table, and a stage at the far end. People were milling around. Dress ranged from dinner jackets to jeans, from long skirts to shirts, tights, and no skirts at all.

Rosie and I, pretty well covered by mid-level clothing, fit in just fine.

About a hundred people were already there, and more were filtering in past the Valkyrie at the door. I recognized some faces from the speech, one of them belonging to the graduate student who had introduced Joe Richmond that night. Rosie said hello to a couple of people, and introduced me to a red-haired young woman who taught art somewhere and was a partner in a video company called Cleo's Asp. Her name was Cassandra, or maybe it was Pandora.

They got into a conversation about someone I didn't know, so I wandered off toward the refreshment table, up front near the stage. There were two bowls of punch, both with orange slices floating in them. One was labeled nonalcoholic. I tried the other one, which turned out to be a watery sangria.

I was drinking punch and listening to a nearby conversation about deformed ducks at a pesticide-polluted wildlife preserve, when a deep, soft female voice said, "I don't think we've met, have we?"

We definitely had not. She had long dark hair, hot brown eyes, and a quirky smile. She was dressed the way some college women dressed when I was twitching through puberty. The kind of older women I found agonizingly desirable. She was wearing a black turtleneck sweater, a black beret, a wraparound skirt and black tights. I must have stared.

"Have we?" she repeated.

"No. But just for a moment there, you looked familiar. I'm Jake Samson."

She extended her hand and I took it, briefly. "Pamela Sutherland. I saw you come in with Rosie Vicente. I've heard her mention you. I don't think I've seen you at any of our meetings, have I?" She was examining me closely as she spoke, as though she were trying to figure out where I fit in the world and if I fit in hers.

"No. Obviously a mistake on my part."

She smiled coolly, ladled herself a cup of the non-alcoholic, slugged it down, and said, "Maybe I'll see you later. I'm on, now."

The guitar case she retrieved from a chair next to the stage stairs was old and battered. She wasn't old enough to have worn it out herself. But then, she wasn't old enough to be copying the dress of the Beat Generation from memory, either. Maybe she'd been frozen for thirty years and someone else had been using her guitar.

There was a quick burst of applause as she strolled onto the stage, set the instrument case down and snapped it open. She looked around and gestured to someone in the crowd, who clapped his hand to his head in a "Damn, I forgot" gesture, trotted off to another room, and returned carrying a wooden stool, which he handed up to her. She placed it behind the microphone, fiddled with the mike until it shrieked, and said, "Hi." The crowd went wild. Then she unsnapped the case and pulled out a guitar that was only a little less dark with age than the case.

It was an acoustic guitar; the stool was a coffee-house stool.

Pamela's style and her performance were perfect examples of the way cycles work. Everything comes back, but always with kinks, like the original idea had been lying wrinkled in a closet too long. Her bearing was not quite right, and she was a better musician than most of the coffeehouse strummers I remembered. As a woman, she lacked the diffidence of those earlier female folksingers. Her songs were not political in the same way—there were no songs about unions and bosses in her repertoire—but there was a villain, a "they" as in "What Have They Done to the Rain?" By the time she'd gotten to that one, an old favorite of mine, I had rejoined Rosie near the back of the room. The song appeared to be a favorite of Rosie's, too, because I caught a suspect glint of moisture in her eyes, and when the music ended, I was afraid she'd break her hands clapping.

"Sentimental slob," I said.

"Yeah. I tend to get maudlin over life and death."

"Melodramatic, too."

"You don't mean that."

I just smiled at her. She smiled back.

"Didn't I see you talking to Pam before her performance?"

"Just a couple of words. I think she thought I was a ringer for the nuclear-power industry. Direct from Rancho Seco, brought to you by the friendly folks at Pacific Gas and Electric Company."

Pam was being cheered wildly by the dewy-eyed crowd.

I wondered if I could ever believe in even a good

cause that passionately again. It would be fun. Probably even good for the arteries.

Pam was taking her bows, but refused to do an encore. Instead, she introduced a band called Three Mile Island. I could not categorize their music at first, until I heard them singing "Moon Over Bikini," followed by "Love Letters in White Sands." Some of the members of the group had spiked haircuts in various colors; some, including the woman who played bass, had crewcuts. All were dressed in skewed copies of fifties clothing. The tenor sax, for example, had orange spikes and was dressed preppie—chinos, sweater and penny loafers. One guy was wearing white bucks, and had one of those little sacks of white shoe-dusting powder hanging from his belt.

Much to my surprise, Pamela was heading our way. She stopped beside me, nodded at me, nodded at Rosie, and stood listening politely to the group.

They were well into their fourth number when the graduate student I'd remembered from the night of the speech stalked over to Pam and whispered, "This is in very bad taste. I'm surprised at you."

Pamela gave him a lazy-eyed look that spoke of infinite boredom.

"They do a great show, don't they?"

"Pam," he said, "this is not funny."

"Noel," she said, "it's not supposed to be. When you produce a show, you can do it your way." She nodded toward the stage. "People like them, they're good, and we're trying to raise money." It was true. The audience was clearly crazy about Three Mile Island. I thought they were great.

"I don't produce shows."

Again, she gave him the lazy-eyed look, but this

time with one raised eyebrow. For a woman who appeared to be under thirty, she was very good at the decades-of-disdain expression.

Noel grunted and stalked off again. Three Mile Island finished their set and announced an intermission. Rosie got into a conversation with someone and wandered off again, toward the punch, probably.

With perfect timing—was he waiting in the entry?—Joe Richmond appeared at the door and the crowd turned like a sheet in the wind to face the back of the room. He waved his hands, smiled, called out a few greetings, a few names, and was swallowed up in the enthusiasm of his partisans. Pam was smiling, but she didn't join the mob.

"Impressive man," I said. I felt like I had to say something, and "impressive" was the first word that came to mind.

"You don't sound impressed," she said.

"I am. As an observer. I was also impressed by your performance. Very moving. But I'm curious about something."

She cocked her head charmingly, and waited for me to go on.

"How does it happen that someone your age does that particular fifties look so well?"

She laughed. "I do it better than most, don't I? I may be the only one in the folk revival that tries so hard to be authentic. I guess you could say it's just part of my act. But I learned it from a good teacher. My mother was Elmira Sutherland."

It took me a second. "Oh," I said stupidly. *"The* Elmira Sutherland?"

Who was an old-time folksinger and writer of protest and satire songs. She did most of her best work in the fifties, but she wasn't widely known then because a lot of her songs got somehow preempted by the male folksingers of her day. Her particular legend came briefly alive again in the late sixties and early seventies, with proper credits at last. Then, I thought I recalled, she died. And Pam had said her mother "was."

"She was a great woman," I said. "She wrote some great songs. I remember."

"Thank you," Pam said simply. "She was involved in some great demonstrations, too. One of them killed her."

Now *that* I didn't remember. I didn't remember Elmira Sutherland dying in a demonstration. I shook my head, puzzled.

Pam explained. "In the early fifties, a bunch of artists and musicians went out to the desert to protest a nuclear test. They must have been too close to the test site. Every one of them is dead now."

"A lot of them must have gotten pretty old," I protested.

"They all died of cancer. Lung, mostly."

I didn't know what to say to that. For a beautiful person, with a beautiful talent, Pam was pretty damned depressing. I thought she was carrying the Beat image just a little far. I looked away, uncomfortable, and saw Joe Richmond coming toward me, smiling.

Turned out that he was smiling at Pam.

She returned the smile and I felt a moment's jealousy, automatically trying to gauge the degree of intimacy.

He put his arm around her shoulder and gave her a quick, friendly hug.

"Everyone says it's a great show, Pam. Thanks." He turned toward me, looking sociable.

"This is Jake Samson. Jake, Joe Richmond. Jake's an observer, Joe."

He laughed. "Good. Glad to hear it. How do you feel about what you've been observing, Jake?"

I decided to tell him the truth. "I think your ideas make a lot of sense. But politics is politics, isn't it? Doesn't the term imply coming to an accommodation with whatever actually is? I don't have a lot of faith in political organization, in political contests. Lots of screaming and yelling and stupid, petty point-making and all it ever amounts to, in the end, is who gets to take home the cash and the power."

He nodded. "That's right. There's been a lot of dis- agreement in our movement about whether we should enter the electoral process at all. The Greens have run some local candidates but have been pretty leery of anything on a larger scale. That's why we broke away. We wanted to go farther. But even among the Vivos we have some people who don't think we should be going for the governorship yet. We even have a candidate who's running specifically so that, if he's endorsed, he can refuse to run. I think it's a tricky issue. Especially when it comes down to splitting the vote, maybe hurting people in the major parties who feel as we do, winding up with the wrong people in office. Very tricky."

What was wrong with this guy? He wasn't self-righ- teous enough, didn't have the God-is-with-me attitude you expect to hear from a politician, especially a pol- itician with a cause.

I decided to poke him harder. "I seem to remember reading some newspaper stories about the Greens in Germany," I said. "The impression I got was that they're pretty far to the left. Is that where you people stand?"

"I'm afraid the press is simplistic," he said. "The Greens have a slogan: 'Neither right nor left, but in front.' And that's how we feel, too. We advocate non-violence, something neither political extreme understands. And Marxism is as materialistic as capitalism. It's the sanctification of unbridled production that's destroying the world. I don't think any of the old formulas provide the right answers. It would be nice," he said, smiling, "if the workers of the world *would* unite and stop insisting on consuming everything in sight."

I was staring at him. I could hardly believe my ears. Pam was laughing. She threw me a triumphant look.

"How are you going to achieve all this great stuff?" I wanted to know. "With a strong state that will wither away when it's done what it needs to do?"

That cracked him up. "Strong states don't wither away. Not ever. I think you need to read some of our material on grass-roots democracy and small-scale organizing."

"Maybe I will," I said, smiling. I was enjoying the man. "But I try to avoid reading nonfiction. If I'm going to get depressed or pissed off, I figure it's best to do it with fictional characters."

"I'm glad to hear you've managed to avoid reality," Pam said. Her tone was cool. She liked me as long as I didn't mess too much with Richmond. She seemed to be losing patience with me. So was I.

"I keep trying."

At that moment, there was some excitement near the door and a tall, handsome older woman entered with a small entourage. There were some shouts, and a lot of applause.

"Rebecca Gelber," Pam said for my benefit. Richmond's opponent caught his eye and they both smiled and waved. At the next moment, a thin, dry-looking man in a dark suit—now here was a man who actually looked like a butler—came up on our other side and, apologizing for the interruption, asked for "a few words" with Richmond. Richmond looked suddenly very serious, and maybe even a bit tired. "Be right with you, Carl," he said. Then, turning back to me, "I wish you would take a better look at us. We could use more people who think, who don't take anything on faith. You're an original, Jake. So are we."

How could you not like a man who says a thing like that?

Then he shook my hand, told Pam he'd see her later, and moved away. I caught a glimpse of Rosie, in the middle of the circle around Gelber. She was talking to the candidate, and her ears—Rosie's, that is—were pink with joy. Pam touched my arm.

"Listen, Jake, I've got to take care of some business right now, but you're going back to the East Bay later, right?" I nodded. "I wonder if I could beg a ride with you? I came over with someone who's staying in the city." I told her sure, Rosie and I would be delighted. She patted my shoulder, smiled—she liked me again—and went to talk to the graduate student. Then intermission was over, and the aging rock star came on to shrieks of audience happiness. He was pretty good, but not as good as I remembered. The impressionist was better.

4

NOT every woman, or every man for that matter, is capable of appreciating a 1953 blue-and-white Chevy Bel Air. One of the things I'd first liked about Lee—besides the way she talked, looked, and moved—was her admiration for my admirable classic.

But Lee was a problem. Besides a tendency to work ten or twelve hours a day, she also got involved in community projects a lot. She would work herself into a state, sometimes, and drop out of sight for weeks. Of course, I could respect that, and understand it. But I didn't like it much.

So I was pleased when Pam showed good judgment about cars, too.

"Beautiful," she said, standing back a couple of feet to admire it. "I think my mother had one of these."

Rosie slid unobtrusively into the back seat, so Pam took the passenger side next to me. She was quiet going over the bridge, responding briefly to my comments about Three Mile Island, her own performance, and the old rock star. When I said I thought Joe Richmond was one terrific guy, she said, "Yes." Rosie brought up her conversation with Rebecca Gelber, and we got some mileage out of that.

Rosie said she had admired Gelber's work for years and had been thrilled to finally get a chance to talk to her. Not only had Gelber been involved in environmental causes for a long time, she had been one of the early and leading lights of the women's movement back in the sixties. She hadn't spent a lot of time in the spotlight, but she'd dipped at least one hand in everything that had ever amounted to anything. The name had, now that I thought of it, sounded vaguely familiar.

Pam admitted that deciding between Gelber and Richmond had not been easy for her. She didn't say what had finally convinced her. We crossed the bridge and headed for Berkeley. She directed me to the University Avenue exit. I drove all the way up University, turned north to go several blocks, then east again toward the hills. The house was not in anything like the same class as the Pacific Heights mansion, but it was big enough and nice enough. She'd inherited it, she said, from her mother. When she invited us in, I accepted happily, looking at Rosie for confirmation. She seemed to think it was a good idea.

The living room had a big fireplace that projected round like an igloo from the plastered wall. But the look was Southwest. Pueblo? I don't know. All the doorways were rounded arches. The rug was definitely Southwest Indian, the furniture overstuffed and in earth colors. There were two paintings in the living room, both by that guy who paints Indians. I liked the room a lot. She offered us wine, and we sat down.

We didn't stay long. We talked about the Vivos, about the convention that was coming in just a month. Somehow, the way Pam explained it, the Vivo election plan didn't sound quite as ridiculous—not quite—as it had seemed at first. There's a lot of stuff involved in becoming a real party: You have to caucus and choose officers. You have to file formal notice with the secretary of state, who then lets the counties know they should be on the lookout for the number of voters registering as members of your party. If you can register a number equal to 1 percent of the total vote in the last election for governor, you qualify. Or you can go another route, the one the Vivos had tried, and qualify by petition, collecting signatures equal to 10 percent of the total vote. What that all means, though, is you have to convince that many people to actually change their party registration. And if you don't register as a member of a major party, you can't vote in a major party's primary. Tends to keep the old two-party system safe.

The Vivos had managed to have a caucus, but since hardly anyone had ever heard of them, they had a little trouble filling the rest of the requirements. So their candidate would run in November as an independent, not as the candidate of a bona fide party. Much easier route, she explained. All it takes for an individual to qualify as an independent is the signatures of about 150,000 registered voters who think he or she should be allowed to run. No one has to give up being a Democrat or a Republican; no one has to be willing to give up the right to vote in the primaries.

But this was just a first step, Pam said. This campaign would bring them a larger following, would create public confidence in the Vivos. And next time around, they would qualify as a party. Easily.

Pie in the sky by and by, I was thinking.

Pam didn't go on and on about it, though. I was grateful when she asked a few questions about some of the detective work Rosie and I had done. We were fascinating.

I guess she must have liked me. I guess she probably thought I was the greatest detective since Sam Spade. When I thought about it that way, it wasn't too surprising that she called me the next day because she'd found Joe Richmond hanging from her acacia tree.

—5—

PAM came out after making her call to the police, grabbed my arm and turned me away from the hanging man.

"All right, I called them. But tell me what to say. You're a detective. What should I say? About his dying here?"

"Unless you killed him," I said, "you should probably tell them the truth. How about I ask you some questions?" She nodded uncertainly. "First, what was he doing at your house naked?"

"Using the hot tub, I suppose."

"Was he staying here with you?"

"No. In the city. I guess he wanted to get away from the people, and the work . . ."

"You guess? You weren't here?"

"No. I was meeting with some of the campaign workers."

"And he just came over on his own?"

She was sitting in one of her overstuffed couches.

She waved her hand at me in exhausted irritation. "I guess so. He knew he was welcome, when he needed to escape."

"He had a key?"

That really annoyed her. "Of course he did. I'm one of his local campaign managers, for God's sake."

I wasn't so sure that necessarily followed, but I ran out of time. The Berkeley police rang the bell. They were charming, as they always are. I guess they have to be.

The two patrolmen did what they're supposed to do with a crime scene—they kept it safe for the bigger guns and did all the preliminary roping off, tucking away, and checking out.

They hustled Pam and me into separate rooms. I got the kitchen, with a view of the hanging tree. I gave my cop what he asked for—personal information and everything I knew about what had happened to Joe Richmond. I didn't say anything about my conversation with Pam just before they got there. They were handling it all very seriously, treating it like a homicide. But that's the form. I was a cop once, for a while, back in the late sixties in Chicago. Long enough to have gotten a couple of calls like the one these guys had gotten. There was a jumper, took a dive off a high rise on the North Side. I roped off everything I could think of—the sidewalk with corpse, the roof, the stairs, the elevator. We kept all the witnesses and residents nailed down for homicide. Much to my disappointment, it turned out the guy had really jumped.

I wasn't with the force more than another year or so after that. I left the cops, and Chicago, right after the '68 Democratic Convention. Right after the big cops-and-yippies riots. After I'd watched everyone go crazy and bust heads. Including me.

Anyway, I confessed that I had dragged the bench across the yard to peek into Richmond's eyes, and that Pam had used the phone in the room closest to the corpse to call them. I didn't know what phone she'd used to call me.

The homicide guys arrived, and the coroner's man, and the lab people. Richmond was cut down carefully, with the noose still intact around his neck, and hauled away. The homicide detective who talked to me—Sergeant Cotter, his name was—picked up where the uniform had left off and went over some of the same ground, as well. Yes, I had "touched things" at the scene. No, I had neither touched nor seen a suicide note. I said I didn't think they'd find one. Cotter, a large, pale blond man, just looked sleepy-eyed when I volunteered my opinion. Then they hauled Pam and me off to the station to give our formal statements.

Again, we were stuck in separate rooms. Again, my inquisitor was Sergeant Cotter.

"So, Mr. Samson. Would you like a cup of coffee?"

Cotter was being a nice guy, trying to get me to relax. I have to admit I was wound up pretty tight. I didn't think coffee would help but I accepted some anyway. It was something to fiddle with. Smoking may kill you, but it gives you something to do when you feel like you need something to do.

The coffee was terrible, whitened with that artificial stuff they make out of pure cholesterol. It didn't do much to make me feel better.

"Why don't you tell me what happened, from the beginning?" Cotter lit a cigarette. "Okay if I smoke?"

I nodded.

"Want one?"

Of course I wanted one, but it had been several years since I'd had one and I wasn't going to lose it now. I shook my head, and told him that Pam had come home and found her candidate hanging from an acacia. That she had called me. That I had rushed right over and checked to make sure the man was dead. That Pam had called the police.

"Nice synopsis," Cotter said. "Why did she call you before she called the police?"

"You'll have to ask her that, but I guess it's because she was upset. We're friends." That was true in a way, and I sure couldn't tell him she'd called me because I was an unlicensed private detective and she'd gotten scared.

"Uh huh. Friends. And this guy Richmond? What was he doing at her house?"

I explained, as well as I could, about Richmond's campaign, about her part in it.

"And how do you feel about the fact that he was running around her house naked?"

I looked at him, my face as blank as I could make it. "I guess he was taking a hot tub."

"And where was Ms. Sutherland at the time?"

"You'll have to ask her that."

"But she was at home when she called you."

"That's where she found the body."

"And where were you?"

"At home."

We rested, each sipping coffee. "How do you feel about the fact that he was at her house?"

"Fine."

"And how does his wife feel about it? He does have a wife?"

"I have no idea."

"Where were you this morning? Until Ms. Sutherland called you?"

"I was having brunch with a friend until a little before she called. She called about fifteen minutes after I got home." All true. Rosie was the friend.

He poked around in my brain some more, and I told him what I could about Richmond and about the Vivo party. He asked me if I knew anything that might have caused the man to kill himself.

That was a tough question, since Pam and I seemed to be suspects. Still, we both had alibis, and I decided to say what I thought. Maybe that would make me less suspect.

"I don't know any reason. People worshipped the guy. He was running for governor."

Cotter looked skeptical, and I could almost hear his cop's mind working. Yes, he was running for governor. In a campaign that couldn't win. A weirdo campaign. And he ran around naked at other people's houses. Women's houses.

He let me go, telling me he'd be in touch.

The thing was, everything pointed to suicide. The weapon, the rope, was right there at the scene, wrapped around his neck. The stool he'd kicked over was right there. It certainly looked like the guy had done it to himself. But the answers, as far as the police were concerned, would lie in the autopsy and in any information they could collect about Richmond's state of mind.

I went back to Pam's place with her. We huddled in the living room, away from the hanging tree, away from the police barriers. There was still a guy scraping around in the yard. Half the house had been dusted. We drank some burgundy and talked, softly, about our interrogations.

"Once they stop suspecting you and me," Pam said, "they're going to decide he killed himself, Jake."

"They've still got a way to go before anyone can say that," I insisted. "The coroner will be able to tell. He's the one who says it's suicide. Or not."

"I don't care what anyone says. He didn't do it. And if they say he did, I want you and Rosie to prove otherwise."

A few days later, Rosie and I were in business, working for Pam.

—6—

ONCE the suicide verdict came out of the coroner's office, the police investigation was effectively over. I guess, in a way, I was surprised. I wondered if the police were satisfied, really, that they had gone deep enough. There's such a thing as a psychological autopsy, I know, as well as the chop job they always do on the body.

The press had reacted with some hysteria to Richmond's death, thrilled by what looked like the murder of a fringe party leader. The front-page excitement was matched, for a day or two, by their handling of letters to the editor—like the one the *Chronicle* headlined "Lynching in Berkeley?" But suicide is less sensational than murder, and pathetic as well, and the story died with the verdict.

Pam wanted to meet with Rosie and me right away to kick off the investigation. I put her off for a day. I wanted to do a little preliminary nosing around before I jumped in. Besides which, I had a date with Lee that night and it had been a long time.

Rosie was eager to get started, but she had a job to clean up first, and couldn't get involved full time yet. Between investigations I slop along on her rent and an annuity from my mother. Rosie depends on her carpentry. I would have to start the case myself.

The first thing I needed to do was get some gears turning so I could find out what the cops knew about Richmond's death—the autopsy findings and whatever else they had that convinced them there was nothing more to learn.

I called my buddy Hal Winter, hoping I could impose on him to do a little snooping for me once again. Hal's a Berkeley attorney with connections in the DA's office. He doesn't owe me a thing. But we've been friends for years, and he once said he was keeping books on the favors he does for me. One of these days he'll collect. One of these days I'll find a way to pay him back.

He was in his office, but he was on another line and could he call me right back? Sure, I said.

I popped a beer and sat on my front steps in the sun. The morning fog was breaking up and the first noontime rays were coming through. The house was chilly, the sun was warm.

I was thinking about Pam. About how she'd found the body. About their friendship or whatever it was. About her alibi, which seemed good. We'd check it out, just as a matter of form. Sure, she was the one who was insisting he hadn't killed himself—a pretty stupid move for a murderer. But just on the off chance that she was totally nuts, which is always possible, we'd check it out.

The phone rang. It was Hal.

"Don't tell me," he said. "Let me guess. Why don't you get yourself a license and admit you're doing this stuff, Jake-o?"

"Do you have any idea what a guy has to go through to get a P.I. license?"

"No."

"Neither do I. Look, I know I already owe you. Let me owe you one more."

He sighed. "When I get it back, I'm going to get it back good."

"Sure, you bet you are, anything you say. It's about that guy named Joe Richmond. The politician."

"Oh, yeah. The guy who bumped himself off in an ecologically sound manner. Something to do with a tree, I believe?"

"That's the one." I explained what I wanted— information about the coroner's report.

"It was a suicide," Hal said. "The guy hanged himself. Right?"

"That's what the cops think."

"And somebody with money to burn thinks otherwise."

"So do I." At least I thought I did.

"Well, I'll see what I can get. When do you need it?"

"It's kind of important, but . . ."

"Cute. I'll try to get back to you this afternoon. I think I can squeeze it into my overloaded workday. If not, first thing tomorrow."

"Thanks, pal."

"Sure, buddy."

I was going to have to find some way to pay him back real soon.

I took my half-can of beer and strolled up to the vegetable garden.

I guess I'd better describe my lot. When I first bought it, there was a big unfenced front yard that consisted of a dirt driveway and a vegetable garden. Behind that were a couple of acacia trees and a 500-square-foot building that not even the realtor dared describe as a cottage. A previous tenant, a lover of plants but no lover of plants in pots, had let the Algerian ivy grow through the walls, roof and floors. It was very pretty.

Behind that was the front yard of what was called, by the real-estate agent, "the house." This was a 600-square-foot stucco box made up of four tiny rooms and a pantry.

There are some big differences now. The driveway is gravel. The front is fenced, to meet the neighbors' fences on either side, and I put in some roses. There are two more trees and a lot more flowers—mostly geraniums, which I don't like much but are easy to grow—back around the house. The house now has three rooms and a pantry, and a Franklin fireplace in the doubled but still small living room.

I lucked out on the cottage. Among the prospective tenants who came to look at it—most of them turned pale even though I was practically giving it away "until the roof is fixed"—was Rosie Vicente. We struck a deal. She'd rebuild the charming, tree-and-rose-draped hovel for a big reduction in rent over the time of remodeling. Then the rent would begin to move up toward market. At first I was skeptical. I had never met a woman carpenter and wondered if she was strong enough to do the work. I wondered if she knew what she was doing. Rosie dated women instead of men and was good-looking enough to disturb my equilibrium, too. Could we be friends? Could we keep our deal? It turned out she was strong enough and knew what she was doing. The deal worked just fine. The cottage is still a little lopsided, because we decided not to replace all the walls, but it's solid and it's pretty and the inside is paneled with real pine and the sun shines in the skylights and the Franklin stove she installed heats the place perfectly all winter.

And Rosie is one of the best friends I've ever had. So go figure.

Anyway, I strolled up to the vegetable garden, a good place for rumination. For a couple of years, Rosie and I tried to be farmers. Here was this big plot of great soil, right? We grew everything we could think of. The cabbages went first, because the snails loved them so much. Then we tried to stop growing potatoes, because they took up too much room and we never got enough potatoes per plant. Tried, I say, because once you've grown potatoes, they're there forever. Then we gave up the beets and the rutabagas because we didn't eat them. Then the bell peppers. Then the onions, because why not buy them?

This year, along with the potatoes, we're down to zucchini, Italian beans, tomatoes, corn, a couple of jalapeño peppers, and brussels sprouts. Yes, brussels sprouts. If you can get them to grow, you can harvest for months. Rosie put in an apple tree and some boysenberries way back at the ambitious beginning, and those produce. So that's the garden. One of these years one of us is going to put in a bench and a little pond full of goldfish. As soon as I figure out a way to keep Tigris and Euphrates from going fishing. Maybe ten years from now, when they've died of old age and I'm married and not so busy chasing women.

The thing I like about the garden is, it's calming. When my head is spinning and I can't figure out why I'm doing what I'm doing and where the hell I'm going next, I go up and look at the food growing. Maybe pull some weeds or water-spray some aphids or pick some snails. I don't think about anything when I'm doing that and sometimes not thinking about anything is the best thing you can do. So I picked some snails off the two-week-old bean plants, put them in a bag, and took them down to the landscaped austerity of the condominiums on the corner. I wished the little bastards a happy and fulfilled life and took my empty bag back home again.

Rosie's truck was parked in the driveway. She and her standard poodle, Alice B. Toklas, were home from work and sitting on her little front deck.

"I've been thinking about the Richmond case," I said.

"Come on in."

I sat on her new futon, she took the rocking chair.

"We need to start writing out a plan of attack, Rosie. The funeral's in two days in Minneapolis—his hometown. Can you go?"

She shook her head. "No. I won't be finished with this job by then."

"Okay. I'll plan on going. It should be a pretty useful trip. With any luck, the other candidates will be there and I'll be able to take a look at them. And family. Pam says there is a wife. Maybe while I'm gone, you can get to some of the local people, if you have the time."

She nodded. "I've already started that." We laid plans for about an hour, then I wandered back to the house.

There was a message on my machine from Hal. He had some information and why didn't I call him back?

He was still in his office. He picked up the phone himself.

"Hi, Hal. What did you get?"

"Oh, hi. Yeah. Well, on the Richmond thing, the guy hanged himself. He definitely died by hanging, by asphyxiation. I got some notes here. . . 'Postmortem lividity in the head, the arms and the lower legs.' The head because of the rope, the legs and arms because of gravity. 'Petechial hemorrhages in the lining of the eyes and eyelids'—that's these little spotty hemorrhages from asphyxiation. Then there was a deep groove from the rope on the guy's neck, and inside that groove there were black-and-blue marks—that means the blood vessels were ruptured by the hanging, which means that he was alive when he was hanged. Nobody killed him first. He'd been dead no more than a couple of hours. Pretty classic, the man told me."

"Maybe. Was there a note? I haven't seen anything about a suicide note in the papers."

"He said there wasn't."

"So what else do they have that makes them call it a suicide? There was nothing wrong with the man's state of mind, no indication he was going to kill himself."

"Well, Jake, I'll tell you, they don't seem to think a whole lot of his state of mind, generally speaking. I

mean the guy was running for governor as an independent, for Christ's sake. Spending all that money
and time and energy. And I guess they did a quick
check on his private life. Doesn't sound like he had
the best marriage in the world. Maybe there was
more, maybe the man had some trouble in his past or
something. If there was more, I didn't hear about it.
That's all I got. Hope it helps."

"It does. Thanks."

We said goodbye.

It didn't help. Not really. I still didn't know why
someone had killed Joe Richmond, and I especially
didn't know how they had done it.

7

LEE and I were sitting in one of our favorite restaurants in Petaluma, which is one of my favorite towns, but things weren't going very well.

I'd been through Lee's moods before and we'd worked around them okay. They were usually connected with work. But this time was different. She didn't complain about a judge or the work-load distribution at her law firm. She said she was fine and work was fine. She insisted that I tell her all about the case I was working on. I told her.

"How do you feel about the party?" she asked quietly.

I hesitated. "They seem like a good bunch of people. Dedicated."

"How do you feel about their dedication?"

What was she after, anyway? I looked at her, trying to figure it out, but she wasn't looking at me, so I couldn't pick anything up.

"It's a good cause. I think their dedication is admirable." The waiter appeared to take our order. We both went with the Pacific red snapper.

"So you think their dedication is admirable," she said, picking up where we'd left off.

"Yeah. What do you want me to say?" I was trying not to get annoyed. "That I'm upset by what's happening to the world? Of course I am."

"Do you know," she said deliberately, "that one refinery dumps millions of gallons of chemical poison into San Francisco Bay every day?"

"Well, yes," I said, slugging down half a bottle of beer. "As a matter of fact, I do know that. And do you know that they monitor that shit by means of some kind of fish that could live in a tank of Lysol? Because when they use other kinds of fish they get something like 95 percent dead ones? I read that in the paper or something. Maybe it was on TV. It was one of those what-the-hell's-going-on-here stories you never hear anything about again. You want me to say I can't believe these disgusting things are really going on? I can't. Okay?"

"What are you doing about it?"

I finished my beer, glaring at her. "I send money to every environmental group that sends me a letter. And I don't use poison on my property." She looked at me for a long time. The fish arrived. We began to eat. Fish had not turned out to be a good choice.

Lee had recently joined a group that was trying to protect the Russian River, a source of recreation and drinking water in Sonoma County, from sewage-dumping by the city of Santa Rosa. Her involvement in this admittedly good cause had made it even harder to get together. I understood that what she was doing was important. What I had not understood was that it was going to make her smug.

"That's good," she said finally. "But what are you doing about it?"

I pushed some fish around my plate. She continued to eat. "I don't join groups, Lee. I don't get personally involved in causes. I don't mess with politics. What I do is I solve murders. Murder-solving takes a lot out of me. And I give what I can."

"I suppose you do," she said.

I ordered another beer. I didn't feel like eating. Lee finished her dinner.

Back in the Chevy, before I had a chance to turn the key in the ignition, she put her hand on my shoulder.

"Jake? I'm sorry. I just don't think I'm in the mood to be with anyone tonight. I need to do some thinking. Okay?"

"Sure. I'll take you home." I was disappointed, pissed off, and relieved that we weren't going to try to stretch this misery over a whole evening. I knew we should be trying to talk. About something. But she didn't seem inclined to, and I thought it might be best just to let things slide for a few days.

I walked her up to her door, kissed her on the cheek, and told her I'd call her around the end of the week if that was okay. She gave me a quick kiss on the lips and said that would be fine.

I drove out of Petaluma, down 101 to Marin and the San Rafael–Richmond bridge that would take me across to the East Bay, trying not to think. I didn't succeed. I was thinking about dedication. Chicago, 1968, the Democratic Convention. Politics on both sides. The mayor a petty dictator with more power than he knew how to handle. The cops corrupt, vicious, and spoiling for a fight. The police department, that is. Not all the cops were like that, although enough of them were so that when the mayor said it was okay to bust heads a lot of heads got busted. I was just a kid, a young cop, horrified by the mob scenes, the tear gas, the hate stirred up on both sides. Young enough to be angry because someone was stupid enough or political enough to risk stirring up my fellow cops, to risk massive violence, to toss a lot of idealistic kids into the pot and let it boil. I was scared, too, decked out in my riot gear, waiting for the shit to hit. And when a young kid came at me with a baseball bat, yelling "Pig!" I bashed him with my stick. He went down. I saw a lot of blood. Someone carried him off but I didn't see that part too clearly because I was crying.

I didn't like what political passion could do.

I drove onto the bridge, still trying not to think. I had told Lee the truth. I give a lot of money to ecological and animal welfare causes. What I didn't tell her was that I never read the stuff they send me. I can't. One look at a baby seal getting bashed or a wolf in a trap or a cat in a lab cage, one word about trees and fish and birds dying in a polluted wildlife sanctuary, one paragraph about the loss of ozone or food irradiation or factory farming, and I can't think about anything else for days. And here I was, driving the wrong way on the Richmond–San Rafael bridge. East. Away from the pretty hills of Marin County, into Richmond, where the hillsides are pimpled with the squat pastel cylinders of refineries. Or maybe it would be more accurate to say tumored. I knew perfectly well that we were heading for shorter living through chemistry, that I might even be one of those people who died an early death.

People who actually get involved in these causes must be made differently from me. They must be able to deal with horror, and with the inevitable frustration. Because I just don't think they can win against the money and the power. As for me, as I told Lee, I do what I can. But doing what I can does not include spending my life getting my head and my heart bashed in. There's a reason why people in the throes of a cause radiate an almost sexual heat. The reason is, politics and love are the same damned thing.

I didn't sleep too well that night; anger always gets in the way of sleep for me. Did I need this shit? No, I did not.

I crawled out of bed around nine, fed the cats, and decided to blow some bucks on a nice breakfast at a café on College Avenue. It was just a few blocks, so I walked, trying to work out some of the tension kinks left over from the night before.

The home fries, soft scrambled eggs, sausage and toast had me feeling better, and I was ready for a day of foundation-laying work. Rosie and I were going to Pam's that night to work out our agreement and do some talking. I like to go to meetings with new clients with a little something tucked away in my notes. Sometimes I make lists.

When I got home there was a message on my machine from Lee.

"Jake? I suppose I should wait to tell you this in person. I wasn't sure last night. Now I am. And I don't feel like waiting. I want to say it now. I've decided to get pregnant. What do you think about that?

You won't be able to reach me today, but I'll be home later this evening, after eight o'clock. Why don't you call me?"

I rewound the message and ran it again. She had decided. I erased the message and I was still standing there, staring at the machine, when the phone rang. I was not ready to talk to Lee. When the ringing stopped I turned up the volume, listened to my own message, and, after the beep, Pam's first few words.

"Hi, Jake. I was just calling to firm up a time for tonight—" I got a grip on myself and turned off the machine.

"Pam? Good to hear from you. When did you want us to come over?"

"I thought eight would be good."

"Sounds perfect to me. See you then. Oh, listen, you want to give me the phone numbers of some of Richmond's family in Minneapolis?"

"I've got his wife's family and his mother. Hold on." She was back in just a minute with two phone numbers. I wrote them down and we said good-bye.

If I didn't get home too late from Pam's, I figured, I would call Lee back and find out what the hell she was talking about.

—8—

ROSIE and I arrived at Pam's exactly at eight. The evening was chilly, and smoke was coming from her chimney, drifting over the top of the avocado tree in the front yard. Pam came to the door in navy blue sweats. She had a wineglass in her hand and offered us a drink.

I accepted a mineral water, Rosie a beer. There were pretzels, crackers and cheese on the coffee table.

She sat us down on the tan couch facing the fireplace and took the matching chair set at right angles to it. She turned her head away and looked at the fire.

"We've only talked a little about the work you two have done in the past," she said. "But you said you've solved a murder or two, isn't that right?"

"Four," Rosie said. "Four murders."

"Good." She turned back to us. The firelight gave her face the color it was lacking, made her look less tired and drawn. Richmond's death was having a powerful effect on her.

"Pam," I began. "You seem very sure that someone killed him. I can understand that. No matter how much I tell myself that the law says it was suicide and the law has reasons to say so, I can't quite believe it, can't quite feel that he would. But you're sure he didn't. Maybe you'd better tell us why."

"I'll tell you," she said, turning her head away again, "if you keep it in strictest confidence."

"We can't necessarily promise that," Rosie said. "When it's over, when the story comes out, we may not have perfect control over what becomes public."

Pam grasped her wineglass and brought it halfway to her mouth, looking down into the last few drops of pale yellow liquid. "You have to promise that you'll do everything you can."

"Sure," I said. "So what's the big secret?"

"It's not that it's such a big secret, really," she said, stalling. "It's just that we had decided. When the election was over, he was going to leave her. Leave his wife. We had just decided that, the night before, on the way to the benefit, and he was happy."

I was remembering that Pam had needed a ride home because she had gone into the city with someone who was staying on that side of the bay. I also remembered the "friendly" hug I'd seen them exchange. "How long had you been seeing each other?"

"About six months." She sighed. "His marriage wasn't good." Then, almost defiantly, "But we would have been happy."

"And of course you didn't tell the police any of that," Rosie said gently.

"No. Vivo doesn't need that kind of publicity now."

I blew up. "I'm tired of your bullshit, Pam. You call me when you find your lover dead in your house, call me for advice and help, and you don't tell me the truth about why he's there! And you don't tell the police he was happy and wouldn't have killed himself because a love-nest scandal would hurt the party? Come on! People didn't blame the Democrats when Gary Hart got caught with his pants down. They blamed him. It could have hurt Richmond, but he's dead. He can't run anyway."

She started to say something but I was too pissed off to stop. "So you let the cops think he was a suicide, instead of telling the truth, but you don't really want to leave it that way, right? Now you're hiring us to dig up the dirt and prove that the man was murdered. What are you leaving out, Pam? When are you going to make sense?"

Rosie nodded energetically. "Yeah. Seems to me that a suicide verdict is the least offensive outcome, politically."

I glanced at her, but she didn't meet my eye. Was this my Rosie, this cold political pragmatist? You never know a woman until you're in politics with her.

"Tell it straight, Pam, or hire someone else," I concluded self-righteously.

She shrugged, only partly with exasperation. "Okay. I'll admit I'm torn. It would be simplest to let it stand. And there are some people in the party who would like to do it the simplest way, and let it be. But Joe was . . . oh, shit, I just don't want him remembered as a man who killed himself. A man who couldn't take the pressure, lacked the stability and the strength to stay alive. Because he didn't." Tears came to her eyes and spilled down over her cheeks. She brushed them away.

"Okay. Fine. I'll go along with that for the moment.

Now tell us why you didn't take the police into your confidence."

"Because my being lovers with Joe has nothing to do with the fact that he was murdered—it's only why I know he didn't kill himself. But the police and the press wouldn't see it that way. I'd be all over the place as some kind of fucking Other Woman. Which is even worse, politically—much worse, I think—than getting caught being an unfaithful husband. No one would ever forget. And after we lose this time, I want to run next time. For Congress, maybe. They don't elect tootsies to Congress, you know."

"And you figure your affair is something we can just kind of skirt around, so to speak?" Rosie said.

"I don't see why not."

I nodded. "Maybe so. Unless he was killed for some motive that had to do with you. Are you willing to take that chance?"

"Yes. Because I don't think it's a problem. I think he was killed for political reasons, and the killers need to be exposed."

I wasn't so sure about her thinking, and I didn't have a lot of hope for her political career. A real politician would have let the suicide verdict stand, happily, and gone on to bigger and better things. She was still mucking around in the memory of an affair that was, literally, dead, and worrying about things like political murder.

"Okay," I said. "Let's talk about those political reasons you think someone had for killing him."

So we did. First we talked about Richmond's competition for the endorsement. Rebecca Gelber, of course, our own favorite daughter. Then there was a guy in Sacramento, and a guy who, like Richmond, was based in Los Angeles, she said. I wrote their names down in my little book. James X. Carney, L.A., and Philip Werner, Sacramento. Werner, Pam explained, was running hard for the endorsement, pushing a platform based on large-scale, pesticide-free organic farming.

"The Central Valley," Rosie interjected, "has some big problems."

I had driven through the Central Valley a few times, and I had to agree. I just didn't think we were talking about the same kinds of problems.

"He really wants to be governor," Pam continued. "He's an ambitious man."

"Well, I'd guess that anyone who went to the trouble of running would want to win," I said.

"No, not necessarily." Pam smiled slightly. "James X. doesn't want to be governor. He wants to be endorsed so he can refuse to run."

I remembered Joe Richmond saying something about that. "Tell me more about him," I said.

"See, Jake," Rosie began, "James X. Carney is a Vivo, but he really stands somewhere between us and the Greens. He feels strongly that we should not run a gubernatorial candidate until we've made it as a legitimate party. That we need to get more strength at the local level, get some people in the state legislature. He thinks a governor's race now will squander our resources."

"That seems reasonable," I said.

"Only if you think we have a lot of time left to be prudent and judicious and stand around with our fingers up our noses," Pam said. "There's going to be a big Carney faction at the convention. If they can get him endorsed, there'll be no governor's race for Vivo."

"Quaint," I said. "Why don't they just vote not to have a candidate?"

"It doesn't work that way. The party decided to have the closest thing we can have to a nominating convention. And that's what it's going to be."

I shrugged. What the hell. I never claimed to understand. No matter what kind of politics you have, you get rules for sliding around sideways.

"Are there any big differences in the way the candidates feel about the issues or about the party—besides Carney, I mean?"

"Leanings, maybe. Gelber leans more in the direction of the anti-nuclear movement. Werner, as I said, tends to talk most about farming issues. Joe was most involved in clean air and water. Carney, well, he's into a lot of different environmental things. But I don't know of any big, essential differences in philosophy. They're Vivos. The biggest differences have to do with methods, not goals."

We talked a little more about the personalities involved, but I knew that Rosie and I would have to check those out for ourselves anyway.

"You mentioned there are people in the party who were satisfied with the suicide verdict, wanted it to stand," Rosie said. "How did you find that out? I mean, did you suggest having an investigation and someone said no, or what?"

"Not exactly. I've talked to a couple of people since his death. Rebecca. Noel. I told them both how I felt—that he didn't do it. Rebecca said she didn't think there was anything to be gained by an investigation. Noel said we should let sleeping dogs lie, and that Carl Maddux thought so, too. That's what he said, the little twit. Just those words."

"What about this Noel guy. What's he in the party?"

"Noel and I are—have been—the local Richmond campaign managers. Bay Area."

"Who is this Carl Maddux Noel mentioned?"

"A man with a lot of money and a lot of connections to people with money. He organized a local recipient committee that backed Joe's campaign." I must have looked lost, so she clarified, or tried to. "You've probably heard them called PACs. Political Action Committees. But at the state level, they're called recipient committees. They collect campaign money for candidates." I nodded, half understanding. I figured I'd have to learn more about that later. "That was Carl's house," she went on. "Where the benefit was."

"Carl," I said. "Skinny, dried-up looking guy, middle-aged, dark suit?" I remembered him. He looked like a butler. He was the man who had come up to Richmond when we were talking and asked to have some words with him. Pam said yes, that was Carl Maddux.

"Anyone else express an opinion?"

"James X. called, just to find out what had happened. He didn't get too excited about looking into Joe's death, either."

I didn't think the political crap was getting us anywhere, so I got down to more meaty subjects, or tried to.

"What about his wife? Obviously, this was not the world's happiest marriage. The cops, I hear, thought that was important. But even if he didn't kill himself over her, she might have some connection with his death. What do you know about her? What's she like?"

Pam just shook her head. "I have no idea. I never met her. And he hardly ever even mentioned her. And no one else has ever said anything about her in my hearing, except to wonder why she sits down there in L.A. and never comes out, except to visit her family back in Minnesota. I have heard that she's beautiful. That's pretty much it. Oh, and rich."

Rosie and I talked to Pam for maybe another hour, mostly, I think, to make sure we believed her and wanted to work for her. We got the logistics straight for the morning of the eleventh. She had gone to what she called a "postmortem" meeting in Oakland for the people who had put the benefit together. She had left the house at ten and come home at 12:30, finding Richmond dead and calling me. She said he had not been at her house when she left, and that she thought he might be coming over but he hadn't been sure, the night before, that he could get away.

Rosie and I talked about Pam on the way home. We both more or less thought she was probably okay, but agreed to check her alibi, just in case.

I'd managed to put Lee's peculiar phone message out of my mind for the evening, but it pushed back into my mind as I walked down the path to my house.

Since it was after eleven when I stepped in the door, greeted by the usual starving cats, I decided it would be more polite to call her the next morning. Really.

—9—

MORNING, as it will do in situations like this, came too soon. At 7 A.M. I had a cup of coffee. I dialed her number and stretched the phone cord over to the kitchen table. She answered at three rings.

"I got your message," I said.

"I wonder," she retorted. What I didn't understand was why suddenly she was retorting all over the place instead of saying.

"I don't understand."

"I thought you'd say that."

"Lee, for Christ's sake, knock it off. I understand that you said you were going to get pregnant, that you had decided to get pregnant. What I don't understand is why, first of all, and whether I'm supposed to be the father, and why, if that's the goddamn case, I don't get to have something to say about this goddamn decision."

"And what would you say if you had something to say about it?"

"Just back up, okay? I asked you—three, yeah, three questions and I'm not letting you answer me with one. You drop this on my head in a phone message, for God's sake, and then you want me to play guessing games with you."

She sighed. "All right. Maybe I'm being unfair. What were your questions?"

Great. She couldn't even remember them now. "The first one is, 'Why?'"

"Because it's time. My biological clock says so. If I don't do it soon I won't do it at all. And because I want to."

"Okay. The second question is, 'Am I supposed to be the father?'"

"Only if you feel capable of it."

"What the hell kind of an answer is that?"

"It's my answer."

"Terrific. And the third question is, 'Why the hell don't I have more to say about this decision?'"

"Because I think you're a chickenshit who never makes commitments and I think if I put it to you you'd just hem and haw and stall around and hope I'd forget."

"I have another question. Just exactly what kind of role do you see me playing as a father? Weekend visits or live-in and total support and the PTA?"

"I guess that's something we'd need to talk about. What you'd be willing to do. What your attitude is. What I would want you to do."

"And if I don't agree to be some kind of stud, you find someone else who will be?"

"I guess so."

My mind was racing, but unfortunately it was racing in panicky little circles. I had a thought.

"What about a sperm bank?" I had not long before had cause to become very familiar with the ins and outs of the sperm business, in the course of finding out who offed an employee of one such institution located up on the Sonoma Coast. I was wishing I was up there now.

"Too impersonal. That's not what I want."

"This is extortion."

"No it isn't!"

I couldn't believe it. She actually sounded hurt.

"You're a fucking attorney, Lee, you should be able to recognize extortion when you commit it."

"I wish you could understand."

"I do understand. I understand that you're saying you want to have a baby and if I don't want to have one with you that's the end. Do you think that's fair?"

"Maybe not. But don't you think you're old enough to be able to make a decision about something like this? Don't you think you're old enough to make a commitment to something? Anything?" There was a nasty edge to her voice on that last word.

"Do I have any time to think about it?"

"Sure."

"How much time?"

"I don't know. I'll have to think about that."

"Fine. You think and I'll think. I'll call you in a few days."

"Okay. Talk to you then." She actually sounded cheerful, chirpy. Was she glad I hadn't said no? Or was she glad because she thought I was going to say no? We hung up. Neither one of us had so much as mentioned marriage.

— *10*—

THE Minneapolis–St. Paul International Airport looked just like O'Hare, which looks just like San Francisco's SFO, which looks just like every other airport of any size I've ever been in. There's something hallucinogenic about arriving in a city and not being able to tell it from the city you just left. I would suspect the CIA of playing mind games with us if it weren't so well done.

The illusion was maintained when I exited the dream world; May in the Midwest is a lot like May at home. Warmish, pleasant. For once, in alien territory, I would neither swelter nor freeze.

I climbed into my rental car—some kind of tacky new Pontiac—and checked out the controls. I found some country and western music on the radio and spread open the map of Minneapolis I'd bought in the airport.

I'd been in the city once before, a long time ago, when I was just a kid, on a trip with an aunt and uncle up through Wisconsin and Minnesota, destination Black Hills. All I remembered about it, though, was that there were a lot of lakes.

I was looking for one of those lakes now. It was called Lake of the Isles, which sounded nice. I found it in the southwest quadrant, one of a cluster of four. I was sitting at the southeast edge of town. All I had to do was cut over to the interstate—35—head toward downtown, and turn off at West Lake Street. Actually, I was tempted, first, to head due north and take a look at Lake Nokomis, Lake Hiawatha, and Minnehaha Falls. I'm a sucker for a love story, even one written by Longfellow. But I decided to try to take care of business first and leave the tour for later. I had scheduled three days in Minneapolis. Today I had appointments with Joe's wife and with his mother. Tomorrow was the funeral. Wednesday was for whatever came out of Monday and Tuesday.

The wife was staying at her family home—she and Joe had met and married here eight years ago, just two years before the move to California, according to Pam. The family home, I had been instructed, was just across the road from the lake. I drove halfway around, slowly, taking it all in. Yes, Lake of the Isles had isles. It also had canoes. And it was watched over by some of the most beautiful houses I've ever seen. Big ones, made of stone and brick. Castles and palaces and mansions wearing smug and impeccable expressions on their expensive facades. Pacific Heights mansions in a more gracious setting. All of them faced the serene beauty of the small, perfect lake. They felt safe from dirt and crime. This is a vision out of the past, I thought, a beautiful, safe neighborhood in the heart of a city. The city boy allowed himself to dream for a few seconds, even though he'd already spotted the burglar alarms. Then I woke myself up.

Okay, so this wasn't heaven, either, maybe, but I was jealous as hell of everyone who lived in these houses, people who drove Cords and Bentleys, I guessed. And Rolls Royces. I was jealous of Joe Richmond for being one of these people, until I remembered he was dead, and that what must have been a beautiful life—or was it?—had ended in an ugly death a couple of thousand miles away from Lake of the Isles.

The house was built of big stone slabs. It had an iron entry gate set into a stone archway. Set into the stone was a brass plaque that said Anderson. There was a button beside the gate. I hopped out of my cheap transportation and pushed the button. Half a minute later, the gate swung open. I drove in, about seventy-five feet to the turnaround near the front door, and parked behind a BMW. Big deal, I thought, disappointed. I could see a BMW anytime in my own neighborhood.

As I walked up the steps, the big dark wood front door opened smoothly and a pleasant-looking woman of sixty or so greeted me by name. I had called from the airport and been told to "come along anytime this afternoon" by this same slightly high-pitched voice. When I inquired, on the phone, I was told she was not Mrs. Anderson. The Andersons were out. She was the housekeeper.

So the housekeeper let me in. She did have the caution to put a question mark after "Mr. Samson?" but she seemed to assume I was not there to sell her magazines. I was grateful.

Emily Richmond was sitting in a lounge chair beside the pool, a book with a flowered cover in her hand. A swimming pool is no big deal in California, where lots of middle-class people have them and get to use them most of the year. But in a place like Minneapolis, I guessed, with three warm months a year, a pool represented real luxury.

So did Emily Richmond. She was wearing a loosely belted ankle-length robe, a pearl-gray confection I was pretty sure was silk. I caught a glimpse of swimsuit under it. The day was not warm enough for sunbathing. Either the pool was heated or she was pretending she was home in Southern California. For my benefit, or rather for my non-benefit, still holding the book, she wrapped the robe more securely around herself. Then she stood, and walked over to me. She was tall and slender, five-nine or ten. She transferred the book to her left hand, and held out her right.

I took it for just a second, a long and graceful hand. Even her hair was long and graceful, fine and ash blond, falling down beside one eye, along the curve and angle of cheek. Her eyes were gray, like the robe, and like the eyes of a woman I once loved. Her lips were finely made, not full and not thin, and her nose was long and perfect. She smiled at me, just the tiniest bit, and invited me to sit at a poolside table. The housekeeper was still hovering. Mrs. Richmond asked if I would like some iced tea and I said I would be grateful. The housekeeper was dispatched.

"I'm sorry about your husband," I said. She nodded, a slight tilt of the head, a slight dropping of the eyelids.

"Thank you. You've come a long way to tell me that."

She was serious.

"I don't understand. Didn't you get my phone message? That I'm investigating his death?"

She looked at me, perplexed in a dreamy way. "Yes, but there's nothing to investigate, is there? I mean why would you do that? He killed himself."

"Well, there are some people involved with his campaign who don't think he would do that. So they hired me. Just to check things out."

She nodded. "That explains it."

I looked for some sign of anger that she'd been left out of the decision, left out of the conviction that someone had done her husband in. I saw none. I did see some slight amusement. Our tea arrived. Emily Richmond thanked the servant and dismissed her. I took a long drink.

"Why doesn't it bother you that someone hired me without consulting you?"

"Because I really have no involvement with them. With the campaign."

"Do you mean," I persisted, "that you planned to stay altogether separate from your husband's gubernatorial campaign? Not be with him?"

"It was silly. He couldn't win. Why spend all that time and money and energy for nothing? He knew from the beginning I wouldn't participate."

"Let me see if I understand," I said gently. "The two of you talked it over at the very beginning and you told him you wouldn't work with him on this? How did he react to that?"

"No, Mr. Samson. You don't understand. We never talked it over. There was no need to talk it over. He knew. I don't do public things. I'm a poet. A private person. A solitary person. I find social intercourse painful and exhausting."

She looked at my glass of tea, still half full. I did not take the hint, swallow the rest of it and get the hell out of there. Instead, I played sympathetic.

"I understand. And even so, despite your feelings, he went ahead and began running?"

She smiled that slight smile again. "Not despite my feelings, Mr. Samson. Despite my lack of feelings."

She was stroking the flowered cover of her book, almost tenderly. It looked like one of those jobs the craftsies sell on Telegraph Avenue in Berkeley—a handmade book of blank pages, to be used as a journal. "Your lack of feelings," I echoed. "For your husband?"

"Joe was a wonderful man," she said noncommittally. "He loved me desperately. Actually, people used to say he adored me." Her expression was soft, reminiscent, pleasant. As though the man had been dead a dozen years.

"But how did you feel about him?"

She frowned at me, a change in expression as small as her smile. "I was grateful. When I wanted companionship, he gave it to me. When I didn't, he left me alone. And he didn't have a wife hanging all over him, keeping him from traveling, from his political activities."

"Why did you marry him?" I asked her, taking care to speak very softly. "For his money?"

She laughed, a quick, breathy sound. "The money is mostly mine. He had some. I had more." She was stroking the book again, glancing at my quarter-full glass. This time, I thought she might simply ask me to leave, but the housekeeper appeared at the door.

"Telephone, Mrs. Richmond." With a tiny moue of annoyance, and not a word to me, she glided off into the dimness of the house.

She left the book on the table. I slid it over. Sure enough, it was one of those journal books, bound in board and covered with blue cotton scattered with yellow and purple flowers. I turned to the first page.

This morning
When the fence posts
steamed like dung,
You cried.

I didn't have time to think about that right then. I wanted to read more. The poem on the next page was longer.

This is a weed
growing like
a flower,
and I can never tell
until
the seeds
all blow away.

On the page after that, something slightly more personal:

You know,
I've never been a summer woman
dancing on the beach,
or autumn's silent dignity,
or winter storms
that shriek
and turn to mud,
or spring,
the easy birth of yellow-green.

I was just turning the page when I heard, "Mr. Samson!" and looked up to see Emily Richmond staring at me. She walked easily across the stones of the terrace and whipped the book out of my hand. Her eyes were not hot with anger but very, very cold.

"I did not mind having you ask me questions about my marriage, Mr. Samson," she said through white lips. "But this"—she shook the book at me—"is a ruthless invasion of privacy."

"I'm terribly sorry," I lied. "I had no idea what it was. I thought it was an ordinary book. I was just going to pass the time with it."

"How much did you read?" she demanded.

"Hardly anything. Then I realized—"

She didn't believe me. "Is there anything else you want to know about my husband?"

"Actually, yes. You said he had money. Where did he get it?"

Still standing, she said, "He inherited it. From his family's mill. Richmond Mills. He's a cousin." Pretty big company, I thought; plenty to go around for all the kin. "Anything else?"

"Yes. Why is it that his friends think he was murdered and you seem to think he killed himself?"

"Maybe I knew him better than they did. Or possibly they never saw his depressed side. I certainly did."

Yes, I thought, I'll bet you did. As though she had picked up on that thought, she glared at me. It was the closest thing to a full, human expression I had yet seen.

"One more thing," I said pleasantly. "Where were you the day he died?"

Her face had become nearly blank again. "In my house in Bel Air. By myself."

"Did you spend any time with anyone that day?"

"Only the servants. I hope that's all, Mr. Samson, because you really have exhausted me. I'm going to my room, and I'll ask the housekeeper to see you out."

"Thank you. See you at the funeral?" She was already gone.

The housekeeper saw me out, but not before I ripped a piece of paper out of my notebook, wrote down both my local and Oakland numbers, and stuffed the paper into her plump, firm hand. Just in case Emily decided she wanted to talk to me again about her husband. In a moment of caper fantasy, I wondered if I could manage to break into this house late that night, steal Emily's book, read the whole thing, really try to get a fix on her. But I didn't know which room was hers. Also, I figured the house was probably well wired, and the local police would be very good about calls from Lake of the Isles. Finally, reading that whole book would probably send me into a depression so heavy my plane wouldn't take off on Wednesday.

I have a problem with poetry. I like some of it, sometimes. But it's hard to judge. Once I read a poem I thought was really terrific, and it turned out to be the ravings of a hospitalized schizophrenic. Of course, that doesn't mean the poem wasn't great. To tell you the truth, I don't know what the hell it does mean.

—11—

JOE Richmond's mother lived outside the city in a close-in, rich old suburb, in a monstrous late Victorian with one of those iron fences that look like they're made of spears. The gate was open. I drove in.

The house sat placidly in a nest of shrubs in the middle of an acre or two of perfect lawn. A few big trees covered its rear, just in case the spear fence wasn't enough to protect it from the twentieth century. There was an entry porch, a second-floor balcony above that, and, at roof level, a widow's walk that you could get to only, as far as I could tell, by climbing out the windows of two tall round towers, one at each of the front corners. The left-hand tower had a rooster weather vane at its peak. A hodgepodge of gables stuck out of the roof at various spots, overhung with elaborately carved eaves. In San Francisco, someone would have completed the fantasy with a three-color paint job, but this house was painted white—trim and all.

I left my car in the well-raked gravel drive and crunched up to the walk leading to the front steps. The people in the house pretended they hadn't noticed my arrival until I rang the bell.

An old man wearing a navy blue suit and a navy blue tie with a white shirt answered the door. He had cold blue eyes and a face ironed smooth except for the thousands of wrinkles and micropouches around his eyes.

"Samson," I said. "Mrs. Richmond is expecting me."

He nodded. "Please come this way, Mr. Samson."

He led me down a long, empty hallway—no hall trees or little fancy tables with mirrors over them. No elephant leg umbrella stands, nothing—and through one of those double sliding doors the Victorians used to hide their parlors behind.

"I'll tell Mrs. Richmond you're here," he said. I nodded, looking around the room, which didn't go with the house very well. It was done in French Provincial, with lots of white wood and gilt and pictures of people who looked like George and Martha Washington. A museum exhibit from the wrong century entirely. Even the mantle looked like it had been ripped out of an older house, somewhere outside of Paris, and stuck against the Victorian firebox.

I sat down on a chair that looked pretty sturdy, resisting the temptation to check the seat of my pants for dust, first. On the table next to the chair was a music box with the figures of two little eighteenth-century people perched on top. When you cranked the box, they did a minuet. I was playing with that when Mrs. Richmond senior came in the door.

I had been expecting a dowager type. Gray hair, big bosom with a brooch pinned at her chest, rings, maybe even a cane. I got the rings, but nothing else.

She wore a big square-cut emerald on her right index finger and an even bigger ruby on her left ring finger. She was wearing those sunglasses you can't see through, so I couldn't see her eyes at all, and her eyes, I guessed, would show her age. She had to be at least sixty-five, I reasoned, since Joe had been in his early forties and had, according to Pam, an older brother. Unless she wasn't the mother of the older brother. Maybe she wasn't Joe's mother either? Maybe there was a mistake and she was their sister? My face must have shown my confusion. I stood up.

She smiled. "Mr. Samson? I'm Marietta Richmond. Why don't you explain to me exactly what it is you want to know, and who is paying you to conduct an investigation into my son's death?"

I smiled back. Her teeth were definitely her own, I could see the slightest sag under her chin, but the hair was carefully and expensively dyed a soft brown. Her shapely, firm-looking body was encased in a long, sleeveless form-fitting royal blue dress of some soft cottony fabric. I couldn't see her legs, but the arms were smooth and slender. I wished passionately to see her eyes.

"I'm sorry if I seem to be looking at you too much, Mrs. Richmond," I said. "But I'm finding it hard to believe you were Joe's mother. Not to mention having an even older son."

"You're very sweet, Jake."

"Thank you. And in answer to your questions, my

client is a friend of his, a political connection. And I want to know about his life, what kinds of relationships he had with what kinds of people. My client believes someone killed him. People usually have reasons for killing other people."

She sat down on a love seat. I took the chair I'd been sitting in before she'd arrived.

"Oh, I don't know," she said. "Sometimes people kill just for the pleasure of it." She smiled again. I really wanted to see her eyes.

"I don't think that's what happened here."

The old man in the blue suit came in.

"Would you like something to drink, Jake?"

"Mineral water would be nice. With lime?"

"And an orange soda for me, please, Gerald."

The old man went out of the room again.

"I'm glad you're doing this, Jake. I don't think he killed himself, not for a minute. He was not that kind of man. He was not that kind of child, either."

"Had you thought about hiring an investigator?"

"No. I never thought of it. But I'm glad someone did."

Gerald returned with our drinks. She took a big swallow of her bright orange soda pop. It left a bright orange mustache. A lesser woman would have made excuses, given reasons, been almost apologetic for liking a child's drink. Not this one.

"I suppose you want to know who I think might have done it?"

"Sure." I plucked the lime wedge off the rim of the glass, squeezed it into the water and dropped it in. "I'd like that. I need all the help I can get." I pulled out my notebook and pencil.

"I have no idea." She took another sip of her soda,

and dabbed at her lip with a napkin. She still had an orange mustache. "But there's his wife, of course. And what about that odd woman who was running against him. Gelber, I believe her name is? I met her once. Although I don't think a political opponent is really the answer."

"Why not?"

"Well, it's not like there was any real power to be had by winning the Vivo endorsement." There was an edge of contempt in her voice. Did anyone close to Richmond, except Pam, respect his political career?

"So I guess you didn't think much of his politics?"

If I'd been able to see her damned eyes, I guessed they would have widened. "I admired my son's politics very much, Jake. What I didn't admire was his delusion that he could make a career of them. I don't understand what he was doing. It was the only stupid thing he ever did. Except of course for marrying Emily, but sex is different."

I stayed away from that one. "So you think the motive was personal?"

She smiled over the rim of her glass. "A scorned woman? A betrayed husband? I don't know about that side of my son's life, but I assume he had affairs. God knows his father did. Of course, his father wasn't killed by a jealous husband, he died in a boating accident." She shrugged. "At least I don't think he was killed by a jealous husband."

"His father, you mean."

"Yes. I think you should look into money. There's very big money involved in politics, isn't there? Big contributions, that sort of thing?"

"Yes. Big money, people with lots of money."

"Joe was a very noble character in some ways, Jake.

He had his ideals, his beliefs. But money was also very important to him. Money to live out his ideals. Money to run his campaign. Money to do as he damn well pleased. Very important."

"But he already had a lot of money, didn't he?"

"Oh, yes, And it was very important to him. That's where you should be looking."

"I'll remember that. Who else do you think I should talk to before I leave Minneapolis?"

"I suppose you could talk to his brother." She went to a small side table, took a pen and a piece of paper out of a drawer, wrote down a number, and gave it to me. "This is his home phone." I already had his work number; I'd gotten that from Pam. "Have you talked to Emily? Maybe she knows something I don't, although I doubt it. Other than that . . ." she waved a limp hand and swallowed the last of her orange soda.

"I've talked to Emily."

"In that case . . . this has been very pleasant, Jake." Her smile was coquettish, charming. "But I'm very tired, and I still have to get through the funeral tomorrow."

"Of course," I said, standing. "If I have any other questions, I hope you won't mind if I give you a call?"

"As long as it's after the funeral. And I do want to know what you find out, ultimately." She leaned forward, toward me. "I really do."

"Sure." I gave her a card from the stack I'd taken off the hotel desk. "And here's where I'm staying, in case you come up with any ideas." She took the card and stuck it in an invisible pocket in the long skirt.

"Would you like to see the rest of the house? Gerald can show it to you. I have an art deco room, a Victorian room, a medieval room, a modern room—I have a Mondrian in that one."

"No, thanks just the same. I'll go now."

"I don't want you to feel I'm being inhospitable. I'll be fine, once I've gotten through the funeral."

"Right. Of course you will."

"Gerald will show you out, then."

On my way out behind Gerald, I was wondering what she thought the funeral was going to do for her. Did she think she would stop mourning once the formalities were over? Did she think that once he was buried everything would be okay and she could take off her dark glasses?

— *12*—

PAM had given me a few leads, a few names to start with. The wife, the mother, the cousin who was currently running the mill. The brother. A couple of old friends. Some political connections, including Richmond's campaign manager, who would be in town for the funeral.

By the time I'd finished with Marietta Richmond, it was nearly six o'clock. No one answered at the business numbers I had for the cousin and brother, or at the home number Marietta had given me for her older son. I did manage to reach one old friend—he hadn't known Richmond was dead, and kept repeating, "Hanged? He was hanged?"—the campaign manager and one local political pal. I'd asked the old friend to meet me, but he declined, saying there was nothing he could possibly know about Joe Richmond hanging himself. When I explained that he might not exactly have hanged himself, the man was even more certain he had nothing to say. The campaign manager agreed to meet me for breakfast the next day, and the local political connection said Wednesday was fine.

I went out for a Japanese dinner and a couple of bottles of sake, then I went back to my room, mellow, full of raw fish, tempura and rice, and called Rosie for a consultation. Her carpentry job, she said, would be finished by Wednesday morning.

"I'm really sorry I'm not with you, Jake. Sounds like the Richmond women are a lot of fun."

"Who knows? You may get your chance. Have you managed to get anything done on your end?"

She had, with Pam's help, paid some calls on Pam's immediate neighbors. No one had seen anything the day of Richmond's death. She'd made a couple of phone calls earlier that evening—it was seven o'clock in Oakland—and was getting some idea of what directions we ought to take out there, and who we should be talking to for starters. That was good news. As usual at the beginning of a case, the possibilities are multidirectional and somewhat overwhelming. And narrowing things down is tough. If you're not careful, you can eliminate someone early on who might have had the key to the whole damned thing. In real life, there's no nice, straight literary line that leads right to the killer. I was hoping to do a great deal of narrowing down in Minneapolis.

After I had talked to Rosie, I called Pam. She wasn't there, so I left her a message to get back to me. I had just settled down with one of my favorite sitcoms when she called.

I ran over some of the same ground with her, although I was a bit kinder to Richmond's wife with

Pam than I had been with Rosie. I'm not sure why. And a little less amusing about Richmond's mother.

Pam told me what flight she would be coming in on the next day, for the funeral. We had agreed that she would travel to Minneapolis, first of all because she wanted to be there, and second, because I thought I could probably use some help in identifying the people who showed up and getting a fix on them.

"I can't believe how hard it is to get away," she said. "Everything's in total chaos. People don't know what to do. I'll have to leave again right after the funeral."

I didn't guess that would be a problem, I reassured her. She sounded pretty wired, and maybe glad, in a way, that she was needed at home. I couldn't imagine that she felt all that comfortable about spending time in Richmond's other life.

I went to bed early and got an early start on the next day, but I might as well not have bothered. Neither the cousin nor the brother was at the mill, and, once again, the brother was not answering his home phone. I was meeting the campaign manager at ten, which gave me a little over an hour with him before I had to head out to the airport to get Pam.

—*13*—

RON Lewis seemed like a nice guy, but somehow he didn't fit my image of a campaign manager.

For one thing, he looked unbelievably innocent. He was a youngish—about thirty-five—man of medium height, with plump cheeks, slender figure, and thin hair. His eyes were pale blue and childishly wide. He had picked me up at the motel and taken me to a place he'd heard of where we could get a "real jack and avocado omelet."

I'm not that crazy about omelets, but he was so proud of himself for tracking down the restaurant that I ordered one.

He started talking about how anxious he was to get back to L.A.

"I feel all torn up, you know? And before this, with the campaign, I had to be all over the state. That was great, in a lot of ways, but now . . . I just need to level out."

"Sure. I can understand that." I needed to get him

on the track, even if he was homesick. "We don't have a lot of time, Lewis. I'd like to get some of your ideas on what might have been going on in Richmond's life and in the party that could have led to this."

He poured cream into his coffee, slowly, watching the color change. Then he added a teaspoon of sugar, exactly level.

"I wish I knew, Jake. I don't think he killed himself. I guess you know about him and Pam. And his political career was going straight up. Straight up." He sighed.

I was afraid he was going to start feeling sorry for himself again, so I broke in. "Pam thinks it was a political murder. You must be more knowledgeable about Vivo than nearly anyone else. Give me some of the dirt."

He looked shocked. "Dirt?"

"Oh, come on. There must have been something, more than one something. If he was murdered, and a lot of us seem to think he was, and if the motive was political, which remains to be seen, then what was the motive, and who was motivated? You must have some ideas."

He screwed up his face. I wasn't sure if he was thinking or about to cry. Turned out he was thinking.

"Well, the people who would be motivated, I guess, would be his political opponents."

I drank some of my fresh-squeezed orange juice, waiting.

"So someone either killed him because they wanted an easy road to the endorsement . . ." He finished his omelet. I could see that this kind of thought was tough for him. He was a manager, a salesman. "Or because he was more than just an obstacle."

"That's good. That's good," I crooned encouragingly. "More than just an obstacle?"

"What if," he said softly, leaning forward across the table, "he was actually dangerous to someone? Like if he knew something about someone that could actually destroy them?"

"Are you making this up because it sounds like a mystery or do you actually have some idea of who that might be?" I couldn't help it. I expected him to start talking about the Casbah.

He sat back again and sipped at his coffee. "Very funny, Samson." I wasn't Jake anymore. "But there was one thing . . . I'm not saying I really know anything about it, but he did mention to me once, he had some idea, that Phil Werner was planning to sell out to a major party if he won Vivo's backing."

"Sell out?" I made a quick note in my notebook.

"Negotiate. Promise to bring in a bloc of votes, and money, in exchange for some kind of office for himself. Jump the fence, turn coat, whatever you want to call it."

"Did he say where he got that idea?"

"No. And he wouldn't tell me. Said he didn't have any proof. What if he got some proof?"

Yeah, I thought. What if?

I looked at my watch. We were running out of time. I needed a couple more things from him.

"Listen, Ron, I'm going to have to take off soon. Can I count on your help in this investigation?" He nodded, serious. "If you come up with anything—anything like that about anyone in the party, will you let me know?" He nodded again. "And I hope you understand I have to ask you this, but where were you the morning Richmond was killed?"

He smiled and shook his head. "I understand. I was in the Bay Area—I suppose you already know that." I nodded. Pam had mentioned it. "I was in San Francisco, meeting with some money people most of the day."

"Carl Maddux?"

"No, he wasn't there. But some of the people on his recipient committee." He wrote down their names and where they could be reached. I exchanged his piece of paper for mine—my Oakland phone number.

"In case you come up with anything. What are your plans now, anyway?"

He shrugged. He looked very sad. "I don't really have any. I could get involved in Rebecca's campaign. She's operating as her own campaign manager—she could probably use more help. I don't know. This kind of took the heart out of me, Joe dying."

I tended to believe that Lewis was okay, but at the airport, with five minutes to go before Pam's plane was due, I called Rosie and left a message on her machine, giving her the information she needed to check his alibi.

—14—

PAM looked tired. She gave me a big hug and asked if I thought we might have enough time for a drink before the funeral. I took her flight bag and told her I guessed we could squeeze baggage retrieval, a drink, and the drive to the church into an hour and a half.

"I don't have any more baggage," she said, "and I just feel as if I'd like to sit still for a few minutes. Not be flying or riding or moving in any way at all."

I could understand that, although whenever I fly— something I'm not particularly crazy about doing anymore—I'm happy to get on the ground and just as happy to get away from the airport.

We found the bar and ordered a beer for me and a glass of wine for her.

"I almost didn't make my flight." She took her first sip of wine, sighed, and sat back a little in her plastic chair. "I couldn't get off the phone, last night, even this morning. People calling with last-minute goodbyes, questions, regrets that they couldn't make the trip. When was I coming back? Where was I staying in case they needed to reach me? Was there a number where I could possibly get a message today? I left your hotel number, if that's okay. There was a meeting this morning, and there's another one tomorrow afternoon. Noel wanted to know if I was going to make tomorrow's meeting. I never felt so needed before, certainly not at five o'clock in the morning." She stopped her monologue suddenly, and gazed at me in an oddly helpless, bereft way. I patted her shoulder.

"I guess your people are pretty confused about who to support, that kind of thing." She nodded. I checked my watch. "Want another glass of wine?" She shook her head. I thought the refusal was probably a good thing, since she looked ready to cry already. "So, when are you going back?"

"Six-thirty tonight." We finished our drinks. I called the hotel. There were no messages for either of us. We went to find the car.

"I had breakfast with Ron Lewis this morning," I said. "He told me something about Philip Werner that I wanted to check out with you." I was driving north toward the suburb where Richmond's mother lived. The funeral was at a church not far from her house.

"What was that?" She didn't sound particularly interested.

"He said Richmond thought Phil Werner was planning to sell out. Did Richmond ever say anything like that to you?"

"Yes, but only in passing. He didn't trust him. He said Philip's candidacy was as real as Carney's, but he said all he had was hearsay and his own intuition to back up the charge."

"That was it?"

"That was it, yes."

Well, the hearsay part was interesting, anyway.

We found the church with a good fifteen minutes to spare. Not exactly a miracle of detecting. There were half a dozen cops on the sidewalk holding back a small crowd of photographers and reporters anxious to get a shot of or a word with the bereaved who were being allowed in. I figured the excitement was made up of three equal parts: the local importance of the Richmond name, Joe's way of death, and his latest role as a fringe candidate in crazy California.

The church was spectacular. It was one of those big old Episcopalian jobs. Very respectable, very High. Very aristocratic. I always feel intimidated by ostentatious displays of Christianity. The man at the door let us in when Pam gave her name.

The bronze coffin, nearly buried in flowers, sat on a platform behind and to the right of the pulpit, if that's what it's called in a high-class church.

I spotted Ron Lewis about halfway in, sitting near the aisle. There were two seats in back of him and we took them. Pam whispered hello and Lewis turned around. He seemed happy to see us.

What I needed was a quick course in who was who, and between the two of them I got some of the important answers before the show started. Ron pointed out the mother and wife, who were sitting a row apart up in front. Marietta was turned slightly toward the man next to her, so I could see she was still wearing her sunglasses. Emily, the grieving widow, had her head bowed becomingly.

I told Lewis I'd had the pleasure of meeting both ladies.

He said the tall, delicate-looking man next to Emily

was her brother, and the man sitting next to Marietta, slouched down and barely visible, was Joe's brother, Walter. Richmond's father, Lewis remarked, was long dead. Right, I thought. He of the boating accident. Then there were Emily's parents and assorted cousins on both sides.

I noticed Rebecca Gelber across the aisle and a few rows toward the front, chatting with some people in her row. "I see Gelber," I said. "Where are the other candidates?"

Pam looked around. "There he is," she said. "Phil Werner." I followed her gaze. The candidate from Sacramento was walking down the aisle, alone. He was young looking, but with gray hair. Terrific bearing. Tall, well built. I guessed he was somewhere in his forties and spent a lot of time in hiking boots. He slid into a seat a few rows to the rear and spoke to no one.

"What about James X. Carney?" I rather enjoyed saying his name.

Pam and Lewis scanned the church. Both pronounced L.A.'s other candidate, the reluctant one, absent.

"You think he'll show up?" I asked. Lewis shook his head. The priest was approaching his pulpit. "Aren't people going to think that's peculiar?" Pam smiled and shook her head. Lewis just smiled.

I'd attended a few funerals over the years. The thing that struck me about them was that most of the time, the officiating rabbi or minister didn't seem to have even the slightest acquaintance with the deceased. I could understand that. I knew a rabbi once, but we didn't like each other, and I hadn't been near a synagogue for a long time.

This funeral was different. It turned out the priest really had known Richmond, as a child and as a man. I couldn't imagine having that kind of stability and respectability. I also couldn't imagine that the priest would say anything about who killed the deceased, so, at the risk of being rude, I asked another quick question.

I whispered to Pam, "Who are those people sitting with Rebecca Gelber?" There were several locally active Vivos, she said, and a couple of Gelber's campaign workers from home. I asked her if Werner had brought any of his campaign people, and, after checking out the row where he sat, she said she didn't think so, but she thought she recognized a local Vivo or two sitting near him.

So far I knew one difference between the candidates, besides the obvious ones of sex and geography. He traveled light, she didn't. And Carney didn't travel at all, not for Joe Richmond's funeral, anyway.

The priest continued to say nice things. I used the time to watch people. Emily's parents sat rigid, unmoving, through the whole eulogy. All I ever saw were the backs of two gray heads. Emily's brother sat very close to her. She turned her head once to whisper something to him and I saw that she was very heavily veiled. So heavily that you really couldn't tell just how mournful she was. Marietta, who had been leaning toward her remaining son earlier, was now leaning away from him. She seemed to be crying. I saw her poke a hankie up behind her dark glasses once or twice. Some of the cousins, also, cried.

I had a really good view of Gelber and her people. She dabbed at her eyes from time to time. One of her campaign workers blew his nose once. They all looked sad, but I couldn't tell whether they meant it or not.

I didn't have anything like a good view of Philip Werner. He was off to the side and a few rows behind us, and any prolonged study would have been pretty obvious and probably not acceptable behavior in the middle of a funeral. An occasional quick glance, though, caught him looking, if not heartbroken, very sober.

When the service was over, I told Pam I'd meet her at the car in ten minutes or so and wormed my way through the crowd after Werner, who was moving fast. I caught up to him just as he was starting his car. He was still alone.

"Mr. Werner," I said. "I'd like to have a few words with you sometime today. My name is Samson."

He nodded, pleasant but neutral. "I saw you sitting with Pam. I suppose you're the detective she hired to investigate Joe's death?"

"That's right."

He nodded again. "Catch me out at graveside, we'll set up a time." Then he put the car into drive and pulled away.

Pam and I caught the tail end of the procession and snaked along to the cemetery. I'd seen a few of those, too, and I hadn't been too impressed.

South of San Francisco there's a town with more dead inhabitants than live ones. That's because it has so many graveyards—big ones—inside its limits. Acre upon acre, a crowded supermarket, or maybe it's more like a bargain basement, of the dead.

None of that for Joe Richmond. Oak Grove was pretty big. I guess most cemeteries are. But it had rolling hills and old trees, big, expensive carved head-stones, statues of angels hovering over the dear de-parted, and several large family tombs for corpses whose names anyone anywhere in the country would recognize. Mostly names connected with food, this being Minnesota. It also had, on this day, some pri-vate uniformed cops that kept the few newspeople who had bothered to come this far at a respectful dis-tance.

The Richmond family mausoleum was nestled in some big trees, oaks, I think, and there were a lot of flowers around it. Rosebushes and a border of an-nuals. The roses were very well cared for. Not a sign of mildew or black spot, diseases I have been forced to think of as ornamental in my own self-reliant yard.

Joe Richmond's coffin was sitting up on yet another platform, this one in front of the mausoleum en-trance. The crowd at the funeral had been fairly large, but only a couple dozen people had come all the way out to the cemetery. There was the bereaved wife, who must have been blinded either by tears or veils, because her brother was steering her around. He looked even more delicate out of doors than he had in the church. Their parents tottered behind. Then there were a few of the Richmond relatives: his mother was still wearing her sunglasses, and his brother looked grief-stricken and angry at the same time. Two weeping cousins stood with them.

Rebecca had driven out with her small entourage. Philip Werner stood with them, next to Rebecca.

Pam was close beside me, almost touching, during the brief service. Ron Lewis stood with us. Aside from the minister actually having known the dead man, this funeral was providing yet another first. I've never been to one where the deceased went anywhere but in a hole in the ground. I watched, fascinated, while they carried that expensive box into the mausoleum. Then the party broke up. On the way back to the cars I got Pam to introduce me to Richmond's brother, Walter, and asked him if we could have a talk later. He looked at me like I'd just danced out from under a toadstool but said I could reach him at home after seven that night and gave me his phone number. I thanked him. Then I caught Werner before he ducked into his car again, and reminded him about our talk.

He scribbled the name and number of his hotel on the back of a card that had nothing printed on it but his name and a Sacramento address and phone number.

"But I won't be back there for an hour or two," he said.

"Fine. I'll call you then. Some time after six." I handed him my hotel card. "In case there's a problem."

Pam was catching a 6:30 flight back to San Francisco, so I drove her out to the airport where we had a decent if unimaginative dinner, patted her on the shoulder, and said I'd see her in a couple of days. Then I called Werner's hotel. He'd checked out. There was no message for anyone named Samson. There was no message at my hotel, either. No wonder the guy traveled light. He liked to make quick getaways.

So much for avoiding a trip to Sacramento.

Richmond's brother, however, was reachable where he'd said he would be, but he didn't want me to go there. He gave me directions to a bar he said was trendy but comfortable. I agreed to meet him there in half an hour.

— *15* —

WALTER Richmond was already there, sitting in a booth near the door, drinking what looked like a double bourbon and water. I slid in across from him, he nodded, I nodded, a waitress in tight jeans and an immense sweater appeared instantly and took my order. The place had shiny pine floors, wainscoting of the same wood, and stark white textured plaster walls. The booths were old and small, dark wood with chips and initials, and obviously came from an entirely different establishment. But the service was good, the waitress was good-looking, and the draft beer was terrific. Couldn't ask for anything more than that. Except a prettier companion.

Where Joe Richmond had been a startlingly handsome man, something had gone askew with Walter, the older brother. His pale brown hair looked like he had trouble slicking it down. His eyes, blue like his brother's, were watery-looking and just a little small and close-set. The family jaw, strong and clean-lined in the second child, was just big and bony in the unrefined version. And most important, where the younger man had looked intelligent and visionary, Walter looked vague and self-absorbed.

"Were you and your brother very close?" I asked, by way of an opener.

"We were five years apart." He lit a cigarette and sucked on it. "When you're kids, that's a big difference."

"So I guess you're saying you weren't close?"

He shrugged. "We didn't start out that way, but we grew up, got married, lived in the same town. Family things. You get closer. We got so we could talk sometimes. Of course, then he moved to California, took over the office out there. You know how it is."

I didn't know how it was, because I was an only child. Walter didn't sound like he knew how it was, either.

"I guess you both inherited money from your father? He's dead, right?"

"Well, yes, but we had our own money before then. Each of us, when we were twenty-one, came into some. The family . . ." He let his words drift off. I drifted with him for a moment.

"Who gets his, now?"

He looked startled, then confused, as if he'd never thought of that. "Wife, I guess. I don't know. We never talked about our wills. Whoever he left it to. I don't know. Why? I don't get all this. Didn't the police decide he killed himself? Who hired you, anyway?"

"Do you think he killed himself?"

He smashed his cigarette into the ashtray, breaking it. Somehow, on him, this was not a violent act but merely a clumsy one. He took a couple of swallows of his drink. His face turned red. "I suppose you think I should have hired someone? Someone to investigate his death?"

"Only if you thought there was a reason to hire someone. Did you?"

He looked down at the table. I wasn't sure, but I thought I saw tears in his eyes. "I guess I thought he must have killed himself, because the police said so. They did an autopsy. I thought they must know. I suppose I'm not a very decisive man, in some ways. But I don't really think he killed himself. Have you met his wife?" I nodded. "Did she talk about him at all?" I nodded again. "I don't think he would have killed himself over that marriage. Even when we were kids, if Joe couldn't have something he wanted, he'd find something else to want. And I don't know why else he would have done it. I don't know much about his political life. I never could understand that crazy Vivo stuff. If he wanted political office, he could have run as a Democrat. All that money for a lost cause. And all that work. He was out to get his heart broken, that's all. Like marrying that damned woman. Stubborn, I guess. If something was easy, or comfortable, he didn't want it. I wanted him to work here, in the business with me, but he wanted to run the Los Angeles office, and then he didn't even want to do that . . ."

Once again, he drifted off. He finished his drink and sat staring into the glass. Tears were rolling down his cheeks.

"I loved my brother, Mr. Samson. I was jealous of him, but I loved him. And it was hard to stay jealous of him, because he was always making life so damned hard on himself. I wish I could have helped him more. I should have hired someone to investigate his death, shouldn't I?"

"It's been done. I'll take care of it."

"Can I contribute? Pay you something extra? Cover some of the expenses?"

I finished my beer and ordered another one. I looked at his glass. He shook his head.

"I have a client, Mr. Richmond. I'll ask her if she wants to accept a contribution from you."

"Thank you."

I stayed with the man for another hour and listened to him talk about Joe, the perfect man who insisted on going after the impossible. The perfect man who never could explain adequately to his adoring brother why he did the things he did. Walter Richmond loved his dead brother, all right, but he wasn't sure why.

I was thoroughly depressed by ten o'clock, muttered something about jet lag, said good-bye, and headed back to my motel.

The elevator was empty when I got in and pushed the button for three so I was alone with my thoughts, which insisted on sticking to Joe's brother. What a pathetic wretch the guy was. I was thinking that I would talk to Pam, when I got home, about letting him toss some money into the kitty for Rosie and me. There was no reason why someone in Joe's family shouldn't contribute something, and he was the one who seemed most interested in the idea. Well, maybe interested wasn't exactly the right word.

I got off on my floor, still thinking about the manufacture of guilt, and as I got near my door, I heard the phone ringing inside and hurriedly jammed my key in the lock, pushed the door open, and, I suppose, reached for the wall switch. I say suppose because I don't remember that part. Something came down hard on my head, I know that, and when I didn't sink to my knees fast enough, it came down again, harder. I was sure I would die, if only from the pain.

—16—

I was lying down in a pool under an icy waterfall. My head was turned to the side that didn't hurt. I was naked and cold and I couldn't move. I opened my eyes. They filled with water. I opened my mouth wide to yell, but all that came out was a choking, drowned gurgle. I spat, coughing, took a deep breath and choked again. I turned my head farther to the side.

Something sawed at my throat and the water I was lying in flowed into my right nostril. Snorting, I blew it out again. I turned my head halfway back, the way it had been at first. More sawing at my neck but that was the best position. Only some water from overhead went into my left nostril, and none flowed in from the side.

I felt sick and weak and the pain in my head was frightening. My vision was washed by a haze of cold water I kept trying to blink away. Everything looked white. I closed my eyes, just to rest. I knew my mind was working faster than it seemed to be, that the reasoning process that seemed to be taking hours was taking seconds. But gradually, in those seconds, my understanding of where I was and why I was immobilized took shape. Naked, my face and chest battered by an icy waterfall, in an icy pool. Although I could turn my head to the side, I couldn't raise it; I was strapped down by a cord around my neck. My hands were tied to something over my head, and they were numb. My feet were bound together. I opened my eyes one more time and tried to get a look around. My hands were tied to knobs that came out of the wall. Knobs, coming out of the wall, above a shiny metal spigot. A small white pool with smooth sides and water pouring down from the shower head forty feet, no four feet, over my face. I could feel the movement of water behind my head. Some of it, at least, was going down the drain my neck was strapped to, but the water level in the tub was not sinking. I lay very still and tried to feel what was happening. I thought the level was actually rising slightly. I jerked against the cord wrapped around my neck, choked, and banged my head on the tub. The bad part of my head. I got lost in the pain and in an anesthetic word game about my head swimming, and how it was too bad it couldn't. I was breathing in gasps, turning my head just enough to avoid the shower's direct hit and still not submerge. A deep breath, hold it, another deep breath, cough on the water inhaled, breathe shallowly to catch up, aim my face to the side and take another deep breath. Good. I tried to yell again, but it hurt my head and I got another mouthful of water. My throat and nasal passages were raw.

I turned my head to the side away from the wound and jerked at the cord again. Just the movement alone was enough this time to make my head ring, and now my neck hurt too.

I began to pull at the cords binding my dead hands. I held my breath; peering through the cataract, I could see three knobs. My hands were tied to the right—my right—and the center. I made myself stop and think. My right would be the hot water. There was none of that in what was coming down on me. The one in the middle was sure to be the one that controlled the shower. If I turned that one off, the spigot would gush right over my face. I jerked at my right hand, the stronger, trying to pull it loose. Asleep, it was hard to control. I jerked again, with no results, and concentrated on moving my hands and arms in their limited spaces, trying to get the circulation back. I turned my head and took a watery breath and gave a feeble yell. Then I jerked my hand against its rope again, burning my wrist. Again. It felt like I'd drawn blood that time, and when I pulled once more I could feel the rope sawing raw flesh. I tried the left hand, damaging that wrist, finally, too. I pulled cautiously once more against the rope around my neck, took another deep breath, spat out water. I would stay calm. I would study the situation. I looked up through the falling water, squinting.

If I tilted my chin up just a bit, I could see the knobs, the ropes, my hands almost clearly, for a second at a time. What I thought I was seeing didn't make a lot of sense, but I decided to go along with the joke. Stretching, I raised my still-numb left arm higher, bringing my hand up and over. It flopped down to my chest. The cord had been simply looped over the knob. I shook my hand hard, then reached up and, fumbling, turned off the cold water. The shower shut off immediately. The spigot dribbled for a few seconds, then stopped. I wiped my face, breathing deeply, sucking in all that good dry air. I stretched my right arm, and that hand came away from the knob as easily as the left one had. I rubbed my hands together, rubbed my arms, shook them, woke them up, tingling. Then I brought my hands around the back of my neck, and found the end of the cord that was holding my head down. I reached with two fingers inside the drain. A cross of metal, the rope tied to it. I felt more carefully, and pulled on the end of rope. It was tied in a bow. It came loose in my hand. The water was already receding, but very slowly. I sat up, aiming my damaged head away from the spigot, and untied my feet. I hooked an elbow over the edge of the tub and pulled myself up, getting to my knees. I did some more breathing, then I crawled out of the tub. I was shaky but I could stand. There were two big bath towels hanging on the rack. I dried myself with one, rubbing as hard as I could to try to get warm, dabbing gently at my head. Then I dropped the wet towel on the floor and wrapped myself, shivering, in the dry one. I looked back at the tub. Nearly all the water had run out of my torture chamber. It was a bathtub again.

I stumbled over to the sink to check out the damage in the mirror. I didn't look at my battered head right away, though, because there was a message for me written in what looked like black crayon. It was, "I could have killed you."

I studied the writing for a minute. Plain block letters, carefully anonymous. Then I cleaned the mirror and studied my head. A big bump and a smaller bump. The big bump would have been scabbed over if it had gotten a chance. As it was, it was a very clean wound. I wondered when the headache would go away, and considered the wisdom of checking with a doctor before I got back on a plane to go home. Both my wrists were burned, and the right one was slightly bloody. My lungs burned, too, and my throat, and my nose. I seemed otherwise to be okay.

Whoever had undressed me—had that been for fun, I wondered, or humiliation?—had tossed my clothes onto the bed. Everything but the cut-off half of one neatly sliced sock. After I dressed and did a quick scan of the room and bathroom, finding no signs of the effects of anyone but myself, I called the desk.

"Couple of things," I said. "I fell and hit my head and I was wondering if there was a hospital nearby where I could get it checked." Then I had to sit and wait while the clerk got the night manager, who then babbled questions at me. Yes, I had fallen in their room. In the tub, as a matter of fact. No, I was not blaming the hotel. No, I did not need an ambulance. No, I did not need an escort, just a cab and an address to aim for. Yes, I was fine. Stop fretting, no problem. There was something else. My bathtub drain seemed to be stopped up. Could they send someone to take a look at it? I understood that they didn't have plumbers on call late at night. Yes, I also understood that they would make an exception in this case and take care of it immediately. And one more thing: were there any messages for me? I'd heard the phone ringing around ten or ten-thirty, when I was just getting in. He checked. Yes, a Mrs. Richmond had called. A Mrs. Marietta Richmond. She had said to call back at any hour.

"But I really do think you should let me get an ambulance, Mr. Samson."

"How about I write a note for your lawyers saying I declined an ambulance and insisted on a cab?" He sighed, and said he did have a release form, if I wouldn't mind. I said I wouldn't.

He said he'd get me a cab.

Before I went, I put in a call to the elder Mrs. Richmond. She answered.

"Jake! I'd given you up. I hope you were having fun, wherever you were."

"Yeah. A real blast. How can I help you?"

"That's not the point. I've decided to help you. You tell me whatever you think has been left undone when you go back to the Coast, and I'll do it. Or get someone to do it. I think you need an inside person, someone inside the family, don't you?"

"No, I don't." I was having visions of a hanged son and a drowned mother. "This could be dangerous, Marietta. We're dealing with a killer. Is that why you called me earlier? To offer your help?"

"Yes, and I'm going to ignore the fact that you don't want it."

"I'm not going to argue with you right now. I'm on my way out. How about we talk in the morning?" She agreed to that. I grabbed my room key and headed out the door. I wasn't in so much of a hurry to see a doctor, though, that I didn't take the time to check that door out in passing. Sure enough, little scratch marks around the key hole. Someone had picked the lock. And I'd been so busy thinking about poor old Walter and rushing to answer my phone that I hadn't noticed. I wouldn't be that careless again.

I stopped at the desk to sign the man's paper. A cab

was waiting, he said, and he lost interest in me entirely.

The doctor wasn't too interested, either, and said the headache would probably go away sometime the next day. I called another cab and went back to the hotel. When I got to my room door I noticed it was not quite latched.

"Who's in there," I said in my meanest voice, shoving the door wide open, hard, so it banged against the wall.

A guy in overalls with the hotel's name embroidered on the pocket stepped out of the bathroom.

"Plumber, Mr. Samson." I guessed that was probably true. "I've already found the problem." He walked back into the bathroom and I followed him. He pointed at the edge of the tub, where, draped and dripping, hung my missing half-sock. "Now how do you suppose that got stuffed down the tub drain?" he wanted to know.

I told him I had no idea.

—17—

BY the time my plane left Wednesday afternoon I'd put in another full day's work, headache and all.

I got up at seven-thirty, had breakfast in the hotel coffee shop, and called Marietta Richmond, since I'd promised I would talk to her again before I left. I was told by whoever answered the phone that she was not available, by which I assumed he meant she was still lolling around in her bed. Was it Victorian? Directoire? Possibly Greco-Roman?

Then I dialed the office number of the cousin who was the CEO of Richmond Mills. I had to go through two watchdogs before I got to the inner office. I would have had a nicer morning if they hadn't put me through.

"Francis Richmond here," a deep, authoritative voice said. "What can I do for you, Mr. Samson?"

I explained once again that I was investigating Joe Richmond's death and was looking for any information I could get from the people who knew him best. I asked if I could stop by the office and talk to him for half an hour or so.

"No, I don't think so. I'm very busy today, and I don't think there's anything I could tell you. I've hardly spoken to the man in three years. I'm sorry if he killed himself. I'm sorry if someone killed him. But I couldn't begin to even guess what might have happened."

"Three years? I guess he wasn't still running your L.A. office, then?"

Curtly: "He lost interest."

"I don't believe you were at the funeral, were you?" I asked. "I don't remember anyone pointing you out to me."

"No, Mr. Samson, I was not."

"Sounds like there was a problem between you and your cousin."

"There was. He was out to hamstring industry, and he was doing it with money that came from our mill. I didn't like his politics and I thought he'd turned into a self-righteous prig. Anything else? I've got a meeting in two minutes."

"Yes. Where were you July 11?"

The man laughed. "At a conference in Chicago. I'll transfer you back to my administrative assistant. She can give you the particulars. Goodbye, Mr. Samson."

So that was cousin number one.

I had just gotten off the phone when I got a call from Marietta. She laughed when I gave her a quick rundown of cousin Francis's thoughts.

"He always was a bastard. But a good executive. I don't think he would have killed my son. He wouldn't take the time. Did you want to talk to any more relatives?"

"Not very much. But if I have time . . ."

She gave me the names and numbers of some people she thought might still have kept in contact with her son. Then she promised to keep in touch. I said I hoped she'd stay out of the investigation. Again, she laughed. She had been right. Now that the funeral was over, she was feeling better.

I had a couple of hours before my lunch appointment with Richmond's local political buddy, so I called the numbers she'd given me. Two more cousins and a nephew. One of the cousins cried a lot and talked about what a sweet little boy Joe Richmond had been. The nephew admitted he was "politically disappointed" by his uncle's death. I didn't know whether that meant he wanted someone of Joe's beliefs to have political clout or that he wanted some patronage to fall his way when it started being tossed around. The other cousin insisted on seeing me. On the chance that she might actually have something to say, I let myself be dragged out to her upper-middle-class suburb—she hadn't gotten her share of the family's money—for what turned out to be an inquisition. She was one of the cousins who had wept at the funeral.

"So," she said. "You're investigating Joe's death." I nodded. "Did Marietta hire you?" I shook my head. "Emily?" I shook my head again. "Who, then?"

"A political associate of his."

"A woman, I'll bet." I didn't say anything. "Come on, tell me about her. Would you like some coffee?"

"No, I don't have much time. So, what makes you so sure the person who hired me is a woman?"

She laughed and shook her head. "Oh, just a wild guess. Joe and women, peanut butter and jelly."

Except, I thought, for his wife. "Are you saying Joe

had affairs?" His mother had said she assumed he did.

"Oh, I don't know. He kind of had that attitude when he was younger. I don't think people change much."

"What about his marriage?"

She snorted. "What about it? But look, I don't know about any of that. I guess I was kind of hoping you could fill me in a little . . . I loved Joe a lot when we were kids. It matters to me what things were like for him, and who might have killed him." Her eyes filled up. I looked away.

The rest of the interview went pretty much the same way. She kept trying to pry information about Joe Richmond's life out of me, I kept trying to get her to tell me something useful. It was a stalemate. After half an hour, I gave up, extended my condolences, and went back downtown for my lunch date.

It was a nice lunch, and he was a nice guy. He'd known Joe Richmond in the old days when they had both been active in the state's Democratic Farmer-Labor party. He was working now, he said, to get Vivos in the state legislature. He corroborated the cousin's impression that Joe and women were peanut butter and jelly. He hadn't heard anything about any California candidates planning to bolt the party. I did get a line on Joe's political past, though. He'd served a term on the Minneapolis city council and a term in the state legislature before he had gone off to look after the family's West Coast interests, become a Green, and dropped out of the business gradually and finally entirely. The two political friends had met again as Vivos.

"Not much in the way of experience," I said.

"Not as an officeholder, no. A lot of dedication, intelligence and charm, though. He was the best we had."

After lunch, I just had time to drop off the rental car and board my plane. No chance to catch the local sights. I was sorry about Minnehaha Falls. And Lake Hiawatha.

—*18*—

ROSIE picked me up at San Francisco International. We had a lot to catch up on. First, she insisted on a blow-by-blow of everything that had happened in Minneapolis after that first day.

"You want it chronologically?"

"Sure. It's easier that way. We can figure out what was important after that."

I sure as hell hoped we could. The forty-minute drive home didn't give us quite enough time to cover it all; there was the talk with Ron Lewis, and then the entire funeral to get through, including the un-fulfilled promises of Philip Werner. Rosie was very interested in the idea of Werner being a defector.

"I'll be very interested in meeting him. When do you want to go to Sacramento?"

"I don't know that's where he went. He could be campaigning anywhere. We'll have to track him down. Besides, I want a little more general information, a little more background on a lot of things here in town."

"Okay, but I don't think we should let him go too long. He sounds prime to me."

We agreed on that. We also agreed that we needed to talk to James X. Carney, who interested me at least as much as Werner, if only because I was enjoying his personality even before we'd met face to face.

By the time I finished with brother Walter and got to my water torture, we had driven through San Francisco and crossed the Bay Bridge. I tried to make Rosie think my ordeal was funny, but she just wouldn't go for it.

"Why the hell didn't you tell the police?" she wanted to know.

"And get stuck there? What would be the point? You think my pal left fingerprints all over the bathroom? You think maybe someone saw and actually could describe some guy they saw picking my lock? Fat chance. Whoever did it was pretty smooth. Except for having to hit me twice. It would have been a waste of time."

She shrugged. "Okay. I guess. But you're all right?"

"Sure."

She seemed reasonably satisfied with that. She slid her pickup truck into the right lane in front of a red RX7 and took the cutoff to route 24, and, almost immediately, our exit to Fifty-first Street. I was glad to be home, not the least because I still got chilly when I thought of that hotel bathtub. It's also a hell of a lot easier to work on your home ground, where everything, every street, every neighborhood is familiar, where you know what to expect from people who look and talk a certain way.

My '53 Chevy was still in one piece, parked as far up in the driveway as I could get it. Not that anything's ever happened to it before when I've been gone, but it was lovingly restored and I'd be pissed off if some asshole kid with a pellet gun shot out the windshield. I might have to spend some time hunting down the parents who were stupid enough to give the gun to the kid in the first place.

Tigris and Euphrates strolled down the path to meet us, but I didn't go back to the house. All of us, Rosie, me, the cats, and Rosie's dog Alice, settled down at Rosie's cottage for some more talk.

Rosie had been doing more than her carpentry job in the almost three days I'd been gone. She'd checked out Pam's alibi, and Ron Lewis's, too. Pam had been at a meeting all that morning. Lewis had been meeting with Richmond's contributors, or fan club, or PAC, or recipient committee, or whatever the hell it was called. She'd talked to a bunch of Vivo people and had some preliminary notes she wanted to go over with me. She had, she felt, eliminated some people there was no reason to talk to at all, and made a list of those who might have something we needed. On that list was a Gerda Steiner, who, Rosie reminded me, was the Valkyrie who had guarded the door at the benefit. She was also, Rosie said, a former member of *die Grünen*—the Greens—in Germany. Gerda's roommate, Cassandra, was listed, as were Noel the graduate student, money man Carl Maddux, and Rebecca Gelber.

That sounded like a nice crowd for starters. Of the locals, I was particularly interested in Gelber and Maddux and I wanted to get a fix on the political and personal relationships of some of these people before

111

I went trotting down south to talk to Carney or tried to catch the elusive Philip Werner. Werner was just begging to be a major suspect, but he'd keep, I thought. And I like to go to my interrogations as well-armed with background information as possible. I smiled, recalling my interview with the divine Emily. It might have been easier if I'd had some idea of what she was like. Not to mention Naughty Marietta.

Rosie wanted to know what I was smiling about, and I told her, realizing that my mind was dithering because I was very tired. I stood up and stretched. "I need to reacquaint myself with my own bed for an hour or so. How about some dinner after that?"

"Sure. Thai?"

"Great. Any particular one?"

"Lampang's okay." It was right in the neighborhood, and that sounded good to me.

"Okay. See you in a while. If I sleep too long and you get hungry, wake me up."

"I will. Oh, I almost forgot. Pam called me this morning, wants to hear about the rest of your Minneapolis adventures as soon as possible. And I took some of your phone messages up to this morning. Your father called, wants you to call him. He said any time in the next month is fine." We both laughed. My father is a martyr. "Your dentist wants to clean your teeth. And Lee wants you to call her. What's going on, anyway? She sounded weird."

"She ought to sound weird," I snapped. "I'll tell you at dinner. Maybe you can give me some advice, being a woman and all that."

"Yeah, and all that. Right. Every time you screw up your love life you expect me to know how you did it."

She patted me on the behind and sent me off to my

own house. The cats came with me. I dumped some food in their dishes, changed their water, and went to bed.

I heard my phone ringing an hour later, but I was groggy and I didn't want to talk and besides it might be Lee and I wasn't ready, so I let the machine take it. I lay there for another ten minutes, lifted Tigris off my chest, and got up. When I was well-armored in jeans, plaid shirt, sweater and Reeboks, and had brushed my teeth, I pushed the playback button.

It wasn't anyone I thought it would be.

"Jake, dear, this is Marietta Richmond. I just wanted you to know that I'm on the job. I talked to Ron Lewis—did you know Werner was a crook? Well, maybe a crook? And Walter says he's paying for part of your investigation. Is that true? I've been toying with the idea of coming out to visit you in Berkeley— you are in Berkeley, aren't you? Or San Francisco?— for a few days, but it looks as if there's lots to do here. And by the way, I love your message."

I live in Oakland, a fact which people seem to find difficult to remember. And my message says, "Hi, this is Jake Samson. Sorry I wasn't here to take your call. Please leave your name and number and I'll get back to you. Thanks." Very creative.

Rosie was ready and waiting. I gave her the great news about Marietta being hot on the trail of getting herself in trouble and, walking up Lawton to College Avenue, the even more wonderful news about Lee. She laughed and shook her head over Marietta, but the Lee part made her quiet.

Finally, she said, "Are you sure she isn't pregnant already?"

The idea was stunning. I tripped over an uneven square of sidewalk and nearly went down.

"Why wouldn't she say so?"

Rosie shrugged. "I don't know. Maybe she wants to feel like she's giving you a choice."

"I'd better call her soon."

Rosie looked at me sideways. "You mean you weren't planning to?"

"Be a pal, okay?" I whined. "Don't start telling me I should go along with all this cheerfully, impregnate the woman, and live happily ever after."

"You said you wanted advice."

"I do. About how to handle this."

"You mean how to manipulate your way out of it?"

"Not necessarily," I objected.

"I think what you do is going to depend on how you feel about her. Do you know?"

We had reached the door of the restaurant.

"I'm crazy about her," I said, with absolutely no conviction. Rosie sighed.

Rosie ordered the duck. I got red curry chicken. The hot stuff, that makes you sweat and cry.

"Let's talk about the case," I suggested. Work is the best escape from life. So we talked. The biggest lead we had so far, about one notch up from suspicions about Werner, was the attack on me in my hotel room. There was a fairly small list of people who were in Minneapolis who knew where I was staying.

I'd already spent some time on the plane thinking about that. I had left my hotel card with the widow Richmond and Marietta the first day. I had not given a Minneapolis address to Ron Lewis or brother Walter or cousin Francis, the CEO of Richmond Mills. I remembered very well that I had made sure Philip Werner knew where to reach me.

"Didn't you say that Pam gave your hotel number to people back here, too?"

That was true, I had to admit. Which could mean any number of things, including the possibility that someone in the Bay Area had told someone in Minneapolis where to find me.

Our food came, and we shifted the subject to the work we had immediately before us. We figured out who we were going to talk to and in what order. Rosie, it turned out, had not talked to Gerda, but only to Cassandra.

"She's actually pretty strange," Rosie said. "She kept hinting dark hints, telling me to ask Gerda, saying that yes, she, Cassandra, knew many things."

"Oh, God."

"Exactly. So I thought we should go see Gerda first."

I thought that sounded like a good idea. "Is that her real name? Cassandra?"

"Probably not," Rosie said, cutting into her duck. I took a big bite of red curry chicken and began to sweat. It would take a little longer before I started to cry.

— *19*—

GERDA Steiner lived just a few blocks from us. Rosie had set up an appointment that morning while I'd been on the phone with Pam, filling her in on progress and damages so far, checking some facts, and asking her to get in touch with Walter Richmond. I did not call Lee. I did not call my father. I did not call my dentist.

Gerda's house was a converted storefront on one of the side streets west of College Avenue. The display windows were covered on the inside by large sheets of canvas. On one of the canvases someone had painted a large mushroom cloud with the circle-bar symbol for "no" across it. I thought that was a reasonable sentiment. The canvas in the left-hand window was blank, and yellowing around the edges. The glass-paneled door was hung with closed venetian blinds. I knocked.

Gerda was waiting for us.

"Rosie," she said, smiling. "Please come in." The look she gave me was politely blank.

"My name is Jake Samson," I told her. "I'm a friend of Rosie's. And Pam's. We both wanted to talk to you about Joe Richmond."

She nodded slowly. "Ja, you are a policeman? The one who helps Rosie?" We were still standing just inside the door.

"Not a policeman. Rosie's partner. We're investigating privately. For Pam." I had figured out a while ago that it sounds less like I'm pretending to have a license if I say "investigating privately" than if I say I'm a private investigator.

"Have I seen you somewhere? I think maybe so."

"Yes. I was at the benefit. And the meeting a couple of months ago."

"Ja. The benefit. With Rosie. I remember now."

I was getting impatient. "Do you think we could come in and talk to you?"

She laughed. Her left cheek dimpled. "Of course. Forgive me."

She stepped aside and waved us graciously into a single large room that can best be described, I think, as utilitarian. It appeared to be a combination living room and workroom, a big square space that had probably been a neighborhood grocery in the old days. There was, in addition to the covered storefront windows in front, one small, high window on the back wall. At the right rear was a staircase which I guessed led to sleeping quarters and a kitchen upstairs.

The room was painted beige, a color that can be either restful or grungy. In this case, it had been painted beige a good ten years earlier. There was a worn brown corduroy sofa—a sofa bed, I guessed at first glance—with black iron-on patches on the arms, and several chairs in various stages of disintegration. One of those fake-wood coffee tables with metal legs sat in front of the sofa. A floor lamp with a drinks tray halfway up its stalk leaned toward the couch. A single scrap of carpeting, five by five, dirty gold and sculptured, protected the peeling blue linoleum from the coffee table's legs. The chipped beige paint of the walls was covered, here and there, with old posters of various political persuasions. A lot of them had to do with stopping rape. I particularly enjoyed the one that said Disarm Rapists. It looked familiar. I wasn't sure where I'd seen it before. At some date's apartment, I thought, sometime in the late seventies.

The entire left side of the room was taken up with office equipment: a couple of old typewriters, one of them electric; boxes of paper; poster paints and brushes; a four-drawer file cabinet painted pale green. A dozen or so folding chairs were stacked against the wall.

Gerda invited us to sit. I perched on a white plastic armchair. She and Rosie sat on the sofa.

"So. I was glad to know that someone was investigating," Gerda said, "I am very glad. The police are wrong. He was not a suicide." She turned serious blue eyes on me, and for the first time I noticed that she was a good-looking woman. The braid wrapped around her head had somehow distracted me, I guess.

I wanted to ask her why she wore her hair like a Bavarian milkmaid, but I didn't dare; she probably had some kind of belt in some kind of martial art, and I didn't feel like fighting. So I stuck to safer subjects.

"How well did you know Joe Richmond, Gerda?" A safe, ease-into-it kind of question.

"How well?" She sighed. I waited. "Not so well, after all." That sounded interesting. Like it was going somewhere. I waited some more, gazing at the perfect white-gold skin of her face and neck. The silence dragged on. I cracked before Rosie did.

"What do you mean?"

"I mean that we had met many times. We had talked. But I did not get a chance to know him so well. Not so well as I wanted. I would have, I am sure, but there was not enough time."

I studied her. She was looking at me candidly, without the tiniest hint of a smile.

"I don't want to pry," I lied. "But are you saying you wanted to have sex with him and that you think he would have gone along with the idea?"

"Ja."

"What about his marriage?" Rosie asked. She knew as much about his marriage as I did, without actually having met Emily, but I thought I knew where her line of questioning might be leading. "What about his political reputation?"

"Both would be safe with me."

"No, I mean, what about his marriage? Was he in the habit of sleeping with his campaign workers?"

She shrugged and smiled.

"So he slept around," I said.

"You are easily shocked, Mr. Samson."

"I am not," I protested.

She gave me a very sexy smile. I was surprised. My first impression of her, at the benefit, was being tested. I had thought, by the way she had responded to Rosie, and by her generally rather muscular manner, that she might have had little interest in men.

"I would not really say he slept around, not that much," she said carefully. "He simply seemed to be, how shall I say it, available." She leaned toward me. "Would you like something to drink? I have juice. Orange, grapefruit and papaya."

"Orange would be nice," I said. Rosie asked for grapefruit. Gerda sprang to her feet and trotted up the stairs. I heard a refrigerator door open.

"I see why you thought we should talk to her," I said to Rosie. Glasses clinked overhead. The refrigerator door closed. "We need to pin this down a little more." She nodded. Gerda came down the stairs, balancing a tray with three glasses, which she set on the coffee table.

"Has he been available recently?" Rosie asked.

She shook her head, sadly. "He did not seem to be. Not for several months. There were rumors that he had settled on Pamela. All I know is that he was different."

"And so you missed your chance," I said. She laughed and nodded. "Gerda, I have to admit that my first impression of you was not . . ."

"Heterosexual? I am surprised that you would see only one side of me."

I didn't know what to say to that, so I got back to Joe Richmond. "Who were some of his lovers?"

"Mostly I heard rumors. I heard the rumor about Pamela, and I suppose now that it is true, but I am not sure and it does not matter. And rumors without names. But I am sure about Rebecca Gelber."

I had to admit that one got me. That tall, dignified, beautiful woman . . . My first unworthy thought was that the man had eclectic taste. My second unworthy thought was that maybe our tastes were a lot the same. If they were, he definitely would have gone after Gerda. That blond exterior, that pale perfect skin—the more she talked about sex the more she radiated. And the warmer I got.

I had a third unworthy thought. Was I interested because she was German? There was something irresistible about the idea of this nice Jewish boy—who had gone about as far from his nice roots as it's possible to go—with this handsome German woman. Reverse conquest? Hadn't I been trained by a dozen liberated women not to think of sex as conquest? Wasn't it time I got over World War II? I had, after all, once owned a Volkswagen.

"What are you thinking about?" Gerda asked warily. I cannot imagine what expression I had been wearing on my face.

"Cars. Sorry, my mind wandered. You're sure that Joe Richmond had an affair with Rebecca Gelber?"

"I don't know there was an affair, as you say. I heard only that they spent one night together."

"When was that?"

"I think a year ago or so. At a meeting in Chicago."

"You say you heard. Who told you?"

"Sandra."

"Your roommate? Cassandra?"

"Yes."

"And how did she find out?"

"She was in the room next to Rebecca's at the hotel."

"I think we probably need to talk to Sandra."

"She might talk to you. She has been talking to men for three years now."

"That's good," I said.

Gerda looked at her watch, a large, heavy, gold men's job. "She will be home in half an hour, Mr. Samson."

"I'd like you to call me Jake."

She smiled again. "Very well, Jake, then. Would you two like another drink?" She looked directly at me. "Or perhaps I can get you something else?"

I allowed myself to let my eyes narrow just a bit, to give her the slightest hint of that old crooked smile. "I think I've had enough for now," I said. Rosie said she was fine, too. "I did want to ask you, though, why you're so sure he didn't kill himself."

"He was not that kind of man. I understand men"—she smiled again—"and women, too. I know he would not kill himself just as I know you want to make love with me."

I did not look at Rosie. I didn't dare.

"There was something else, too," I said, realizing how silly that sounded in the context of this conversation. "The morning he died, there was a meeting, to talk about the benefit of the night before. Were you there?"

"The meeting was here. I was here. And as I told Rosie, Pamela was here, too."

"And who else?"

She named her roommate and several people I had never heard of. I asked her to write down their names for me. She went to the electric typewriter and, laboriously, slowly, picked out the list of names. She was just finishing when the front door opened and Cassandra came in.

I remembered her from the benefit, the redhead,

attractive in a distant kind of way. She worked in video. I stood up and she asked me to sit.

She said hi to Rosie and greeted me by name. That was nice.

Gerda pulled her list out of the typewriter and brought it to me.

"Sandra, Jake and Rosie want to hear about the night you saw Rebecca and Joe together."

Cassandra looked at me appraisingly. "I don't know if I want to tell you about that. Will you use it against Rebecca?"

"Only if she killed Joe Richmond."

"Don't be silly." She sat down on the couch with the other two women. "Well, what can I say? They were together. It was a national organizational meeting in Chicago. My room was next to Rebecca's. I got in late, and as I was walking down the hall, I saw Joe go into her room, carrying a bottle of wine. He was in there all night. I could hear them. Her bed was up against the same wall mine touched. I could hear them, and I could hear the bed. Just like a man. They can't be trusted to be faithful."

I did not say what should have been obvious: Rebecca was married, too.

"And when was this?"

"In November. I guess that's about eight months ago, right?"

It was. Which would make it just about two months before Richmond started his relationship with Pam.

— *20*—

THE town of Benicia is about twenty minutes north of Oakland, just across the Carquinez Strait where the Sacramento River flows through a couple of smaller bays before it empties into the big one. A beautiful little town with quiet pretty streets, Victorian houses, a state recreation area and a historical park.

A lot of artists have moved there in recent years because housing is relatively cheap—in Bay Area terms anyway—crime is low, and the surroundings look pretty and peaceful. An ideal town, in many ways, with a great future as an artist's colony.

I'd consider moving there myself, if it weren't for the refinery upriver and the toxic dump just outside of town. Kind of makes you stop and think.

The Gelber house was on one of the streets that looked like it was made of money. Big homes, big yards. Big-ticket cars. The house next to theirs had a new Mercedes in the driveway. The Gelbers lived more modestly, apparently, and tended toward Berkeleyism. They had a Volvo.

The house was a Victorian, painted the way Marietta Richmond's place should have been—sky blue with two-color trim, white and dark red. Very nice. I parked the Chevy at the curb. It looked good there since it, too, is sky blue and white.

I checked my watch. Five minutes early. I glanced at Rosie's face, which showed intense concentration. I guessed she was squeezing respect and admiration out of her mind so there'd be some room for suspicion and hard questions. Sometimes this is not an easy business. I winked at her as if to say, "No big deal, kiddo, we'll all get over it." Then we walked up the steps to the fern-hung front porch and rang the bell. A cheery, two-note chime.

The man who came to the door was wearing Birkenstock sandals, running shorts with a beeper hooked onto the waistband, and a Sierra Club T-shirt. He was eating a carrot. He was thin, gaunt like a runner, with a lined face and white hair. When he smiled, the lines in his cheeks deepened to crevasses. He transferred the carrot to his left hand, and extended his right, first to Rosie, then to me, saying, "Bruce Gelber. Rebecca's husband. You must be Jake Samson and Rosie Vicente. Come on in." His face was not familiar. I didn't think I had seen him at the benefit and I was sure I had not seen him in Minneapolis.

We followed him into a narrow hallway that opened onto rooms on both sides and led to a kitchen at the back of the house. The hardwood floors looked like dark glass. The walls were bright white. The little hall table with the mirror above it looked like cherry wood that had been aging pleasantly in the homes of the comfortable for a hundred years.

"I'm afraid Rebecca is going to be a few minutes late," Gelber said. "She's meeting with some of our neighbors today. I don't know if you're aware of the ecological issues here in town . . ." As he spoke, he led us into a room that would have been one of the parlors back when Victoria was matronizing half the world. The room was done in mauve and taupe—is that brown?—and various blues and creams. He sat us down in a pair of comfortable chairs.

"I know you have some problems here," I said tactfully.

He nodded sadly. Then he brightened artificially, like a bare light bulb. "Can I get you something? Tea? Coffee? Beer? Wine?" We both asked for beer.

I was glad that we would have some time alone with Rebecca Gelber's husband; I wanted to know more about him, how he felt about the party and his wife's place in it. And how he felt about Richmond. I wondered if he had any idea that his wife had been charmed by the possibly terminally charming Joe Richmond.

Gelber trotted out of the room and trotted back in seconds later with three beer bottles. German beer. He handed one to me and one to Rosie.

"So," I said, when he had sat down on a mauve love seat, crossed his legs, and taken a sip of beer. "What do you think about all this?"

He looked uncertain for a moment, as well he might, but the confusion didn't last long. "I was shocked about Joe. Horrified. I don't know what to think. But you two are the detectives. Seems to me that the real question is, what do you think?"

"I try not to," I replied, smiling cryptically. Rosie was sitting quietly, sipping her beer, watching Gelber in that analytical way she has that would scare me to death if I were the object. "Mostly I'm wondering what this is going to mean to your wife. And to the campaign. And for that matter, to you. I guess I've been curious to meet you. Husband of the candidate. What's that like, anyway?" I was using my best man-to-man voice, and he responded.

"I'm very, very proud of her," he intoned. "It's not every man who has a chance to know a woman like Rebecca, let alone be married to her. I only hope that being a woman doesn't limit how far she goes."

That sounded like a prepared speech and could have been at least partly for Rosie's benefit, so I pushed a little farther. "Yeah, but it probably will. Are you heavily involved in the party? I didn't see you at the benefit—do you just stay out of it? I could see where you might . . ."

He gave me a thoughtful look. "I am involved in the party. At least as much as I can be. I'm a very busy man with a heavy schedule. Surgery. Surgical oncology. We're a two-career family."

And I can't figure out whether you like it that way, I thought.

"I guess that's why you didn't make it to Richmond's funeral."

"I felt badly about him. He was a fine man. I would have liked to be part of that ritual. But my patients usually can't wait. And of course he was Rebecca's professional connection, not mine."

I sipped my beer and squinted at him, trying to see if there was any hint of anger or irony in that last statement. I couldn't spot a thing. Maybe Rosie had been able to.

"Do you think Richmond's death puts your wife in front at the convention?" Rosie asked.

"It should, but I don't know if it will. There's Werner to be contended with."

"What do you think of him?"

"He's competent."

Rosie pushed on. "Do you want her to be endorsed?"

He shook his gray head at her. "What I want is hardly the point. If the party endorses her, she'll run."

"But of course you don't expect her to win," I said.

"No. And that's the pity of it. Not this time, anyway."

"So you wouldn't mind? About maybe becoming California's first gentleman someday?" I said it, Rosie didn't. I didn't think she could have without gagging.

I might have liked the guy if he'd had the grace to laugh, but he didn't.

"I wouldn't put it that way, Jake. I don't know where you're coming from with a question like that, but the answer's easy. I would love to see my wife—my partner—in the governor's mansion. She deserves it."

"And you'd be living there, too, of course. Not a bad place to be, right?"

He did smile at that, but he turned his face slightly away from me and his eyes rested on a spot somewhere to my left. "Possibly you are more power-oriented than I am, Jake. I assure you that medicine is more than enough for me."

I guess Rosie decided it was time to change the subject, because she asked the alibi question. "I hope you don't mind my asking this, Mr. Gelber, but you understand we have to know the whereabouts of everyone even distantly connected with Richmond on the morning of his death. Could you give us some idea of where you were, who you were with, that sort of thing?"

He nodded earnestly. "Of course. Let me get my book." He got up and left the room.

"I don't like him," Rosie said softly.

"I hardly ever like doctors," I said. Gelber had failed to convince me that he had no interest in political power. For one thing, he was the one who had brought up the word *power*. For another, I figured that a doctor who specialized in cancer surgery must feel pretty helpless sometimes. A little control over a large state could go a long way toward alleviating that troublesome feeling of impotence. I didn't have long to think, though. I was just getting to the part of my thought process where I decide that everything I've thought up until then is wrong when Rebecca Gelber strode into the room looking magnificent and apologizing for being late.

Both of us leapt to our feet. I was struck again by the beauty of the woman. A classic kind of beauty, dignified and graceful and timeless as a Greek sculpture. An aging Athena. I had guessed when I'd first seen her, across a room, that she was in her late forties. Now I could see that mid-fifties was more like it. What I couldn't figure out was what she was doing married to a guy like Gelber. I had to remind myself that I'd never spoken to her, and that some of the classiest-looking women I'd ever met had been pretty boring.

Besides, I could hardly ever figure out what anybody saw in anybody—or I could see it too well.

Just as she and Rosie were saying their hellos, and I was being introduced, Gelber slid back into the room carrying an appointment book, skidded to a halt, smiled blindingly, advanced, kissed his wife on the cheek and said, "I didn't hear you come in, Rebecca. How did it go?"

"Fine. Everything's fine. I told Howard that you'd call him about the petition."

She sounded abrupt, or maybe just tired. Gelber caught the tone, and nodded. "I'll do that now, and leave you alone to talk. Mr. Samson? You asked where I was the morning of the eleventh? I had brunch with my wife, then, at eleven, I went bicycling with a friend."

"Could we have your friend's name?" Rosie asked.

He looked annoyed. "Sure. Mack Frazier. Doctor. Do you want his phone number?"

"Yes, please." I scribbled the name and number in my notebook. "Thanks very much. Sorry to trouble you."

"No trouble," he said, still annoyed. "Pleasure meeting you both." He didn't mean it. He left the room.

Rebecca turned back to us. "Please sit down." She glanced at my empty bottle and Rosie's half-empty. "Would you like another beer?"

We declined and sat down again.

She started to sit on the love seat where her husband had sat, then changed her mind. "I think I'll just have a glass of wine, if you don't mind waiting for another second." She was tired. Her smile lined her face and made her eyes look sad.

I watched her walk out of the room. She was wearing a white jacket and pants that looked tailored and expensive. Her walk was firm, shoulders back, with no trace of weariness. I guessed she could hide it everywhere but her face. I've noticed that starts happening somewhere around the age of forty. Years of faking it wear the face out first.

She came back, sat down, and started asking me questions.

"Why are you checking up on my husband?" she wanted to know. She spoke pleasantly, with mild curiosity. "Do you suspect him of something?"

"Not really," I said blandly. "We just need a picture of what everyone was doing the day Richmond was killed."

She laughed and sipped her wine. "Isn't that the same thing? I'm afraid I don't have an alibi beyond that brunch with my husband. I spent the rest of the day alone. I had a campaign dinner scheduled for that evening, but then I heard about Joe."

"Who told you?" Rosie asked.

"One of my campaign people. He'd talked to Ron Lewis. You know Ron?" I nodded.

"And what time was it that you talked to him?" Rosie persisted, determined to find an alibi in there somewhere.

"Not until right before the dinner. About five." She sat back, rubbed her neck, drank some more wine. "I suppose you're wondering about my relationship with Joe? How I felt about running against him? What I thought of him as a candidate? Possibly you want to know how I felt about him personally?"

"Yeah," I said. "Those are some of the things we've been wondering. But let's start at the beginning. Do you think we really have something to look into? That he didn't just kill himself?"

She shook her head. "That's hard to say. I suppose that you've been talking to a lot of our people. And that none of them think he could or would kill himself?"

Another question. I wanted her to answer in answers.

"Most of the people I've talked to don't think so. For various reasons. But what about you?"

She laughed softly. "All right—may I call you Jake?—I'll tell you what I think. It's what I told the police. I think he could have killed himself. I think he was essentially unhappy. He wasn't happy in his marriage, he wasn't happy that he had no children, and he wasn't happy with his . . . social life."

"Don't be so coy—may I call you Rebecca?—and please do call me Jake. I know he chased women."

She looked at me, her gray eyes soft and sadly amused. "I don't know that I would put it exactly that way, Jake. He didn't have to chase women. They chased him."

It was hard for me to say, but I said it.

"You, too?"

The soft eyes went hard and blank. "I'm married, Jake. Happily."

"Rebecca, someone saw you."

"Someone has a vivid imagination." She drank the rest of her wine. "I'll be happy to give you any facts I might have that could help your investigation, but I'm not going to play games with you. Joe and I respected each other, even liked each other. Whoever said we slept together was lying."

It seemed to me she was taking the "lie" awfully

seriously. It made her angry. There could have been any number of reasons for that. She could have been concerned about the political effects such a story might have. She could have been worried about its effects on her marriage. Or maybe she was angry because it was true. I was tending toward the last reason, mostly because she was staring so blankly at me. One of those direct, honest gazes out of Orphan Annie eyes. A gaze that reminded me of my ex-wife, who was a pretty good liar, especially when it came to this very subject—whom she had and had not slept with. I dragged myself away from that comparison. I wanted to continue liking Rebecca Gelber.

"Look, Rebecca," I said. "At the risk of having you hate me, I'd like to pursue that subject for just a while longer. It doesn't matter to me whether you and Joe had an affair, except that it would help me to understand both of you a little better. I am very interested in the man's private life. He's dead, and I think someone killed him. I need to find out why. Sex is one hell of a motive—from disappointed lovers to pissed-off husbands. And I'm going to find out the truth one way or another. I'd rather not have to keep asking other people. I'd rather get something that feels true from you, right now. Your husband doesn't have to know—if he doesn't already."

She glanced at her empty wineglass, sighed, and looked at me with those soft, sad eyes I'd seen earlier. "You are a persistently insulting little bastard, aren't you?" But she was smiling, almost affectionately, when she said it. "I suppose it's common knowledge?"

"I don't know. I heard it from one person." She nodded thoughtfully.

"I think it's probably common knowledge. But as

far as I know, Bruce is unaware. And it really has no significance of any kind. It was a fluke. An infatuation that lasted a few days. We were away from home. The meeting was exciting, full of promise for the future. We were up, happy . . . he wasn't happy very often in those days."

"What about you?" Rosie asked quietly.

"You two are merciless, aren't you?"

"We try."

She laughed. "I wasn't happy and I wasn't un-happy."

"Then you were bored."

"No. Not really. There was plenty to keep me oc-cupied."

"So you two were high on politics, excited about the same things, fell into bed. Okay. How did you feel afterward?" I probed.

She studied me for a moment. One corner of her mouth went up. Her eyelids drooped. I felt the heat rise. "Sleepy," she said.

"I mean how did you feel when he took someone else to bed, showed interest in other women?"

She was still smiling quirkily. She knew she'd gotten to me. "I expected it and I was relieved. Really. Of course, there was a twinge of jealousy. I think there always is unless the experience is totally repellent. But it really didn't matter to me. Is that enough of that subject?"

"Not quite. You say you knew he was with other women. Which women? How did they take his love 'em and leave 'em ways?"

"Oh, I think you're misunderstanding Joe. It wasn't that way. He honestly cared about everyone. He did not have a Don Juan attitude. He expressed his affection."

"Just a sweet, simple guy, right?"

"Well, sweet anyway. And attractive. And sexy."

"And about one inch deep."

"Are you married?"

"No."

"Monogamously involved?"

"Not exactly. Okay, okay. Forget it." I couldn't help but laugh. She'd gotten me again. "Tell us about some of his women."

"I only know of two others, for sure. Pam and Gerda. And I have no idea how they felt about him, or how far things actually went with them. I suspect he and Pam were still seeing each other when he died."

"If you don't mind," I said, "I think I would like that second beer, now." I needed some time to breathe and we still had questions that needed answering. She asked if Rosie wanted one. Again, Rosie declined. Rebecca left the room.

She'd given in and told the truth about her affair with Richmond, but she was such a clever woman that I couldn't be sure the whole process hadn't been planned. Maybe she had not made a big show of telling the truth so we'd believe the rest of what she said—that she had felt just fine about getting dumped after a night of passion. Sometimes it's very difficult dealing with people you suspect might be smarter than you are. I prefer feeling superior.

"Let me ask her about Minneapolis," Rosie said. "You're doing too much of the work." I thanked her.

Rebecca came back, handed me the beer, and sat down again. Rosie picked up the questioning.

"You were in Minneapolis for the funeral, right?" Rebecca nodded. "Was your husband there with you?"

"No. He had a full schedule that week. He stayed here."

"Where were you later that night, after the funeral? Say, after—" she glanced at me.

"Ten."

"After ten?"

I was creating an interesting image of this tall, sturdy-looking woman stripping me and tying me down in the shower.

"Well, let's see. I spent the early part of the evening meeting with some local party people, but I think we broke by nine or so. I went back to my hotel and went to sleep. Why? Was someone else killed?"

"Not quite," I said.

Rosie changed the subject to politics.

"His death gives you a better shot at the campaign, doesn't it?"

"A better shot, but hardly a clear one. Phil Werner is the most likely candidate, at this point. Unless someone else appears from out of the blue. In any case, I've still got some very strong competition. It's possible, you know, that James X. will come out on top."

"About Werner," I interjected. "There's a rumor that he'll bolt Vivo if he's nominated. Take all his marbles and try to hand them to a major party. Joe Richmond apparently believed it."

She gazed at me, disturbed and surprised. "I've not

heard anything like that. I know Joe didn't trust him, but—no. I've never heard that. I don't believe it."

"Werner and Carney," Rosie returned to the original subject of relative standings. "Are those men as strong as Joe Richmond?"

"Probably not. But they're men, in any case, and that makes them a little stronger than they would be otherwise." There was no malice, no sulkiness in her voice. She was making an objective political judgment, as far as I could tell.

"What do you think your chances are?" I asked.

"I have a good chance of being endorsed—good to fair, I should say, and no chance at all of being elected."

"What do you really want, then? I mean you as a person, you as a politician?" I was getting interested in spite of myself.

"I want us to make a strong showing. To be recognized as a viable power. To be the magnet for an ecology coalition. To qualify as a party."

"Then what?"

"There's some disagreement about what comes next. Most of us, I hope, want to gather enough support and enough money to win the governorship next time around. Or the time after that. I want us to run people for the legislature, and for Congress. I want us to create a strong national organization and run a presidential candidate. We want change, and we want people in office to make that change happen."

"Well, good luck," I said. "So maybe you could run as an independent this time and lose, and get a Vivo nomination next time and win. Maybe you could run for president in a few years. Does your husband want that, too?"

"Not enough to kill for it, if that's what you're driving at."

It was, but I denied it and repeated the question.

She sighed. "Well, of course he does. Why wouldn't he?"

I must have stared at her. She meant it. This incredibly intelligent woman apparently saw no reason why her husband might not want to be the first gentleman of California, or even of the country.

"Rebecca," I said. "Look at history. How do you think Pat Nixon liked it?"

It was her turn to look at me as if I were out of my mind. "What in the name of God do you think I have in common with Richard Nixon?" Rosie was grinning. She found that amusing.

"Politics," I said. "The desire for power."

Rebecca didn't get angry. She nodded slowly and gave me a cool but friendly look. "Sometimes," she said, "people are more interested in what they can do with power than in the power itself."

"That's true," I said. "At least that's what they say." I finished my beer. "We won't keep you any longer, but I'd like it if we could talk to you again, Rebecca."

"I'd like to see you again. Both of you. And I'd like to help if I can, although I'm not sure there's anything to help with." She stood. We stood. "Jake, I'm sorry you're convinced you have to act cynical. I'm sorry you've been so disappointed. You must have been quite an idealist once."

I took her hand, pretending to shake it good-bye. "I must have been. But I don't remember."

— *21* —

I don't usually have my poker games on Thursday nights. Unless something really important intervenes, they're on Tuesdays. But since I had been 2,000 miles from home on Tuesday, I'd put it off a couple of days.

I'd also managed to put off until Thursday the return call to Lee. Her answering machine informed me she was not available but would call me back. I told it that I would not be available after eight o'clock that night but would be around first thing in the morning.

Lee had never come to a poker game, she said because they were always on weeknights instead of the weekend when she felt more free to make the drive. I'd always thought that was too bad, since I think I cut a pretty dashing figure at the poker table. This night, however, I did not think it was too bad. I was glad I did not have to feel obligated to invite her. I needed to relax. Certainly there was something to work out between us, but everyone needs a night off, right?

Hal Winter came. Hal always comes, busy as he is. I'd met Hal in 1976, back when I first moved to the East Bay from Marin County. I met him through a friend who was having a legal battle with his landlord. Hal, a black man, got his start with civil rights and tenant's rights cases. He was a passionate man back then, with real heroes and real enemies, a man with a sense of history. He's still a passionate man, but true to the eighties, he has now moved on to the corporate world, where he is making very good money.

"I think it's my duty," he likes to say enigmatically.

The only thing I don't like about Hal is that he eats like three pigs and stays skinny. He had already swallowed a bowl of corn chips by the time my other old pal, Artie Perrine, showed up.

Artie and I have done each other some favors, too, and we go back a few years. He's an editor at *Probe Magazine,* in San Francisco, and it's his letter of credentials I carry around to legitimize my illegitimate investigations whenever that becomes necessary. The letter says I do freelance work for the magazine. Artie's idea was that he might get something out of that someday in the form of information for one of *Probe*'s articles. He has, once or twice. He also got free detecting once when his nephew was accused of killing a guy in Mill Valley, where Artie lives.

Hal, Artie and I sat around drinking beer, poking at the fire in the Franklin stove—evenings in the Bay Area are warm only in August and September, if then—and talking. Hal, of course, wanted to know what was happening with the case, and Artie was instantly interested in the possibility of a story on Vivo. I gave them both some bare bones to chew on and admitted that Rosie and I were at the running-in-circles stage. Then we sat around for another few minutes, waiting to see who else would show up. The three of us were the hard core, Rosie played from time to time, and a couple of other people showed up more or less regularly. There'd been only a few weeks when we hadn't come up with at least four, and we usually had five.

Rosie arrived around eight-thirty, with Alice. Alice had a rawhide chewstick, which may be her version of poker. We sat down at the table and I began to count out chips, ten dollars each. We used to play for three, nickel ante. But over the years, we've all gotten a little more solvent, and we were up to a racy dime, quarter, half, instead of the old nickel, dime, quarter. I'll play for more in Tahoe, of course, but this living-room stuff is just a game and a chance to see each other.

We drew for the deal and it was Artie's. He called seven stud.

My hole cards were the two of hearts and the six of spades. First up was queen of diamonds. Hal was showing a five of hearts, Rosie the eight of clubs and Artie the queen of hearts. I, first queen, tossed in a dime. Everyone else thought that was a good idea.

Fourth card, Hal picked up a nine of clubs, Rosie a king of clubs, I got a five of diamonds and Artie gave himself a seven of clubs. Rosie checked. So did I; so did Artie. Hal bet a dime. I decided to stay in because what the hell, this wasn't Tahoe, and nobody else was showing anything all that great.

Third up, Hal was showing five of hearts, nine of clubs, king of diamonds. Rosie had an eight and king of clubs and jack of hearts. I had picked up the four of clubs, which gave me four on an inside straight—whoopee—and Artie gave himself an ace of diamonds, to go with his queen of hearts and his seven of clubs. Hal checked. Rosie checked. I checked. Artie checked. Fourth up: Hal, still nothing showing; Rosie, another club, the three, for three showing on a flush; me, another four for a tiny pair; Artie, another queen. Artie bet a quarter. Hal folded. Rosie folded. I decided not to let him get away with it, and tossed in my bet. Last card, down: nothing to go with my fours. Artie had me beat on the board.

I thought about bluffing, but Artie doesn't cave in too easily and he likes calling my bluffs.

Hal called draw, jacks or better to open. Rosie couldn't do it. I had a pair of queens and assorted garbage, and tossed in my dime. Everyone stayed in. On the draw I took three and got nothing. Rosie bet a quarter. Was she bluffing? I decided yes, and stayed in. Artie folded and so did Hal. Rosie had two pairs, fours and aces. She'd drawn the second ace. I was getting off to a slow start.

Rosie's first deal, she called five card stud, suicide king wild. The suicide king is the king of hearts. Like all the royalty in most decks, he has a pained look on his face. But this guy has a good reason. He's holding a sword and it looks like he's sticking it right through his own head. I don't think it's an accident that the suicide king is the king of hearts. I also didn't think it was an accident that Rosie had suicidal royalty—not to mention the king of hearts—on her mind. Neither of us had been totally convinced by Rebecca Gelber's insistence that her peccadillo with Joe Richmond had meant nothing to her.

I, however, wanted to put the case out of my mind for a couple of hours. I called flip-flop, a really stupid game where you keep choosing one of two cards to show until you have four showing and one in your hand. The one in your hand is wild. I am the only person I know who doesn't hate flip-flop.

The deal went around a couple more times. Then, around ten, the phone rang. I thought about letting the machine catch it. Lee didn't expect me to be home, or answering the phone, I reasoned. Still, she could be trying. And maybe I should answer it. Maybe I was beginning to feel guilty about sidestepping this baby thing. Maybe I didn't like my hand. It wasn't very good. I tossed it in and went to the phone in the bedroom. My message was just about finished. I picked up the receiver and shut off the machine.

"Hello."

"Is this Jake Samson?" The voice was a whisper.

"Yes, it is."

"I have to tell you something." Did the whisper sound familiar?

"And what is it you have to tell me?" I felt silly, talking to Deep Throat on a perfectly normal evening in Oakland.

"They're planning something terrible." The voice sounded female, but it did not have an accent. That let out Gerda, unless she was capable of affecting an American accent. Who the hell was it, anyway?

"Who is? Who's planning something terrible?"

"They're going to sabotage a chemical plant, make it look like a toxic accident. Right before the election."

"Who is? And where is this plant?"

"Some of the people involved with Vivo. So they'll get more votes. I don't know who. Ask Werner."

"Where? Where is the plant?"

"California." She hung up.

It could be someone trying to lead me off in the

wrong direction. It could be true. I went back to the game, thinking I would probably lose a bundle, after this.

Rosie checked my face out pretty thoroughly, maybe looking for signs of impending fatherhood. My expression, I think, must have puzzled her. It was her deal. She gave up staring at me and got down to the matter at hand.

"Five draw, guts to open—in fact, let's make it pass-out—the game of life." Pass-out is a form of draw poker where you can't check before the draw. That means the opener, and everyone else, has to either bet or drop out. No choice—you make a commitment, you put your money where your mouth is, you get right in and get wet or you drop out of the game. That's why Rosie likes to call it the game of life. She's just full of symbolism, I thought bitterly. I don't like the game much because it limits my options. You can't use a ploy that I often use: you can't check and lay back with a strong hand, watching the action and then raising the other players after someone else has opened. And I had a damned strong hand: aces and threes. I opened for a dime, scaring no one off. We drew. I still had two pairs. I checked. Artie made it a dime. Hal and Rosie folded. I raised Artie forty cents. He stuck out his jaw and saw me. All he had was a pair of tens.

It was my deal. I called low hole follow the queen, a game full of wild cards and changes of fortune. Now that's my idea of the game of life.

It was a good evening, despite the phone call. Maybe the surge of adrenaline helped my poker. I made twenty bucks.

It was midnight by the time Hal and Artie left. I

144

stopped Rosie on her way out and dragged her back inside.

"Jesus," she said, after I told her about the call. "I thought you had a funny look on your face. You were kind of gray. You think it might have been a woman but you didn't recognize the voice?"

I shook my head. "Not for sure, not even enough to make a good guess."

Rosie thought about it. "And she said ask Werner . . . that doesn't make a lot of sense. Why would Werner have anything to do with trying to win more votes for Vivo in the election if he's planning to defect after the convention?"

"He might if he thought he was going to lose the endorsement and stick with Vivo for another four years. If he loses, he doesn't have a lot to offer another party."

She looked exhausted by the possibilities. I was, too. We made a breakfast date for the next morning. I left the beer cans, the chip crumbs, and the soggy two-inch remains of the chewstick where they lay, and went to bed.

— *22*—

BEFORE getting started the next day I put in a call to Lee at her office. She wasn't in. She wasn't home, either. I tried calling my father. No answer. My third productive call was to the office of Doctor Mack Frazier, Bruce Gelber's alleged golf partner on the day of Richmond's death. Doctor, I was told, was touring China and would not be back for a month.

After all that success, I went up to the cottage to get Rosie and take her to breakfast. We needed to organize our thinking.

"All fingers point to Werner," Rosie said, stuffing a forkful of home fries into her mouth. I nodded, playing with my soft scrambled eggs. "He must be the key to the whole thing."

"Maybe," I said. "We don't know where he was when Richmond was killed. We don't know where he was when I was given my involuntary shower. And that voice last night . . . the mystery contestant. Ask Werner, it said. And Richmond not trusting him. All that points to him. But it doesn't make sense. If he wants the endorsement as a prize he can run somewhere else with, he doesn't want Vivo getting a lot of votes in the general election. He sure as hell doesn't want a Vivo-backed candidate to win. Why would a defector want the party he left to succeed?"

"We don't know he's planning to defect. We don't know anything about him except that he's probably the front-runner for the nomination and that he avoided talking to you in Minneapolis."

I took a bite of egg and poured some hot sauce over my potatoes. Better. "You're right. That's true. But what about the locals? Rebecca can't account for herself at all, not for the morning of Richmond's death or the night of the attack on me. And who the hell knows where her stringy husband was?" I had told Rosie about the China trip. "Sexual jealousy is the best motive for murder I know. And consider the James X. Carney situation. Here's a guy who doesn't bother to go to the funeral. He's a political opponent. He's fighting Richmond every step of the way, fighting the idea of a gubernatorial candidate. How much does he care? Enough to try to screw up the convention? Enough to knock off the prime candidate?" I had a sudden inspiration. "What if he and Werner are working together? If it's true that Werner's a turncoat and that Carney doesn't want to back a Vivo gubernatorial candidate—think about it. With Richmond out of the way, Werner's the next best candidate."

"But what about the chemical-plant sabotage?"

"A red herring?"

"Sending us to Werner?"

"Well, maybe. So he can lead us off in a wrong direction."

Rosie looked skeptical, with good reason.

We spent some time going over the ground about who was in Minneapolis and who wasn't, who was covered for the morning of Richmond's death and who wasn't.

"His wife was sitting in her house in Bel Air," Rosie said.

"Probably," I agreed.

"Ron Lewis was in a meeting with some money people."

"Pam, Gerda and Cassandra were in a meeting, too, talking over the benefit."

"His mother probably didn't do it."

"Or his brother. And speaking of money people, I'm setting up a meeting for us for this afternoon with Carl Maddux. Pam's tracking him down."

Rosie finished her coffee. "Don't I remember you saying that he wasn't in that meeting with Ron?"

"Yeah."

"I wonder why not. I wonder what he was doing."

I shrugged. "Probably investing in hog futures or something. Who knows what people that rich do with their time."

Rosie laughed. "Let me know when we're going to see him. There's one more left on my original list—Noel Chandler. I think we should see him today, too. Then I think we should do some traveling."

No question about it.

I drove us home. There were three messages on my machine. The first was from Marietta Richmond.

"Jake, dear, this is Marietta. I'm sure you're out doing wonderful things." She paused. I thought I heard her take a swallow of liquid. I could imagine her, lounging in something long and silky, sipping orange soda. I could imagine the orange mustache it left behind, too. "I also have been doing wonderful things. Emily is still staying with her family. I have had someone following her. I can report without any reservation that she goes nowhere and does nothing. But I'll keep trying to catch her. Bye-bye."

The second call was from Pam. We had an appointment with Carl Maddux at his house in Ross—not, she said pointedly, the house in San Francisco—at two o'clock. I called Rosie and told her, so she could try to set things up with Noel.

The third was from Lee. She was now at her office. I called there.

"I've been thinking about it a lot," I said. "And I still don't know what to say. This is a very big thing you're talking about. I can't take it lightly. I can't make a decision just like that. I need to see you and talk to you in person about it."

"Yes. All right. When?"

"That's the problem," I said. I heard her sigh loudly. "No, I mean it. Really. I'm working on a case, you know that. And it may be bigger than just the death of one man." I liked the sound of that. And if the sabotage tip had any truth behind it, the line was true. She sighed again. "I have to leave town for a couple of days. I should be back by Tuesday at the latest. But I may really be in the thick of it by then. I can't just stop working when I'm on the edge of collaring someone."

"God, Samson, you're full of shit."

"No, I'm not. Can we make a tentative date for Wednesday, and I'll try, really try not to put it off?"

"All right. Wednesday. Be at my house at eight, okay?"

"Okay." Or what? If I get there at nine will I find you busy conceiving with the meter reader?

I still had some time, so I dialed my father's number in Chicago again. My stepmother answered.

"Eva! It's me, Jake. How are you? I got a message Pa called."

"Called? Sure he called. Why wouldn't he call? Your father loves you, Jake. I love you. Everything's fine here. Is everything fine there?"

"Yes, fine."

"And how is your tenant, the Italian?"

"She's fine."

"Such a beautiful girl. It's a shame she wears those boots."

My father and stepmother had been out visiting last summer and had met Rosie. Eva had never gotten over Rosie's cowboy boots. As a matter of fact, it was their visit that had led to my meeting Lee. She was a niece of Eva's, and Eva had pushed us together. See what good comes of that sort of thing?

"And Lee? Are you still seeing my beautiful niece?"

"Now and then, Eva."

"What does that mean, now and then?"

"It means sometimes."

She clucked at me. "Such a Mister Cool. Your father wants to talk to you, Mister Cool."

"Okay. Bye, Eva." She was already gone.

"Jake?"

"Hi, Pa. How are you?"

"Fine. You're fine?"

"I'm fine."

"What kind of trouble are you getting into?" I didn't think he was talking about Lee. On that last visit, he had finally figured out that my work could be dangerous—he got a bump on the head himself strolling down my driveway in the dark—and had decided I was involved in something secret. I think he liked the idea and worried all at the same time.

"No trouble, Pa. Taking it easy."

"Liar. You'd be home more if you was taking it easy."

"I gather you've tried to reach me more than once?"

"He gathers. So? I know you can't talk about it. So okay. Just take care of yourself. And Rosie? How is Rosie?"

"Terrific."

"And Lee?"

"Wonderful."

"Okay. That's good." His voice dropped to a whisper. "Don't forget next week is Eva's birthday." Then, louder again, "So, keep in touch more. Don't get hit on the head."

"Good-bye, Pa."

"Good-bye, Jake."

I ordered some flowers to be sent to Eva—I knew if I waited until the next week I'd never remember—and spent a couple of hours going over my notes. I felt like we were getting close to something, but I couldn't figure out exactly what it was.

—— 23 ——

CARL Maddux lived in a town in Marin County where the rich don't have to get richer, they already are.

Ross sits cozily in a heavily populated corridor of Marin, north of Mill Valley, Corte Madera, and Larkspur, tucked along Sir Francis Drake Boulevard on the way to Fairfax.

Sir Francis Drake continues out through the West County, where the landscape grows increasingly rural, and ends at Highway 1, the coast road, at the tiny crossroads town of Olema. That's where you'll find the entrance to the Point Reyes National Seashore. Where you can find some of the most beautiful beaches in the world.

I used to live in Marin County, a long time ago. I ended up there in the early seventies, after some time spent wandering up and down the Coast. I lived in a bunch of those towns at one time or another—in one of them with a woman I was married to for a while.

An ugly story, that one, full of lies and sneaking and meanness. Friends who knew what she was doing and stayed silent, as if silence were a moral stance, as if neutrality had anything to do with friendship. But those were the cool, "you do your thing, I'll do mine" days of doublespeak Me-babble, not too far removed from the hit-on-a-joint, tab of windowpane, laid-back revelations of eternity we'd all wallowed in a couple of years earlier.

What really amazes me is that I still love Marin County, even though I've lived in the East Bay, now, for over a decade. It's beautiful, and the beauty was always there, through all the shit, and maybe kept me sane, or nearly sane, anyway.

People keep telling me, these days, that Marin has gotten tight-assed. Rosie complains that fewer and fewer of those great beaches allow dogs. That does seem to indicate a certain tidy, suburban twist of mind—what's a beach without dogs chasing seagulls and tossed driftwood? And I keep hearing that the kind of people I knew there, the odd ones tucked away in the hills, the poor artists and writers and itinerant carpenters and knights-errant, don't live there anymore because they can't afford to or because the atmosphere is no longer right. Except possibly in the West County towns, San Geronimo, maybe, or Lagunitas. But see, it was always that way in Marin. There was always an "except in." I've been back to a couple of places I used to live in. The houses cost a hundred thousand or so more now than they did then, sure, but that's true in Berkeley, too. And nothing looks all that different.

And I can't ever drive to Marin County without having a small, scared feeling of homecoming.

You can get off the Richmond–San Rafael Bridge right onto Sir Francis Drake, so that's what I did. In about ten minutes, we were cruising through Ross. Maddux lived off Shady Lane, which has nothing to do with naughty ladies. I found the house, even though I couldn't see it from the road, and even the address, out at the mailbox, was hard to read. The front of the property was screened by a ten-foot-tall, dense hedge of prickly, mean-looking holly. The gate was closed, but not locked. It swung back easily and I drove through.

The drive must have been an acre long, if something can be an acre long. It was lined with redwood trees, and they weren't babies. The house was tucked into more trees, but not so many or so big that the rooms got no sun. It was hard to tell how big the place was, because there seemed to be more of it everywhere I looked, behind every bit of native California landscaping. Windows and decks and levels, all in the same, although denatured, redwood that sheltered them.

It was almost like camouflage. The best houses are like that, I think—part of their hill or canyon or ravine. I glanced across the front seat at Rosie. She smiled and raised her eyebrows in appreciation.

I thought I heard a stream running somewhere. Now that was really something. Almost anyone in Marin can have a winter stream, but this was May and it hadn't rained in over a month. Big money.

Of course, I already knew that. We found the door and pushed the bell. I didn't hear anything, but figured that maybe somewhere, deep inside the house, soft chimes played Bach.

Maddux made it to the door in under a minute, so

I guessed he must have been waiting for us. He was dressed more casually than he had been the last time I saw him, in slacks and sweater and open-collar shirt, but he still managed to look inhumanly clean and neat. Of course, I understand that it's easier to look that way if someone else washes and irons your clothes and you have more clothes to start with. But this guy looked like he had someone following him around brushing him off and spot-pressing. I became more aware of the mustard stain on the front of my shirt.

He took us into a medium-sized room of wood and leather and books, with a wall of French doors leading out to a large deck.

We sat on brown leather couches at right angles to each other, Rosie and I on one, he on the other. There was a large decanter on the coffee table, on a tray with brandy snifters. He offered us some; I declined, Rosie accepted. He poured hers, but he didn't pour any for himself.

"It occurred to me after I talked to Pam," he said softly, "that it might have been more convenient for you to visit me in my San Francisco house. I spend several days a week there."

"Oh no. This is fine," I said. "Very pleasant." Pleasant. Like a rustic Taj Mahal. I had remembered that he spoke quietly, and had the nearly invisible quality of an old-fashioned butler. I hadn't remembered the paper-like quality of his skin. Pale, thin, dry, almost powdered-looking. He was thin, too. But he didn't look sick. I was betting he'd looked the same way when he was ten years old. Now? Probably somewhere right around fifty-five or sixty, fifteen or twenty years older than I am. I wanted his money.

"We don't want to take any more of your time than we have to," I said. When you want someone's money, you have to be polite, by way of making up for it.

"I'm sure you won't." He smiled slightly, cracking fault lines all down his cheeks. "I remember seeing both of you at the benefit. I don't remember hearing you were detectives."

"We try not to brag," Rosie said. She doesn't usually come up with wisecracks during interviews. Either she was crazy about this guy and felt instantly comfortable with him, or she didn't like him at all.

He smiled again. "Why don't we begin, then?"

I started out slowly, by asking him some background questions: when and how he'd gotten involved in Vivo; why. Then I went on to some tougher ones, like why he was so involved in putting together money to support a losing candidate.

Maddux had, he said, been a member of various conservation, wildlife, and ecology groups since the sixties. He saw Vivo as being part of an international network that included the Greens, and he had been interested for several years in organizing backing for a major candidate who would represent a new, "relevant" political direction.

"Organizing backing, you said," I interjected. "Exactly what do you mean by that? It has to do with your PAC, right? Your recipient committee? What is that, anyway?"

He nodded ruminatively. "Well, let me see if I can . . . a PAC is a Political Action Committee, a non-party political group."

"You mean like a special-interest group?"

"Not necessarily. On the state level—you seem to already know this—they're called recipient committees, which seems self-explanatory. Committees formed to receive funds for candidates." He smiled humbly. "I don't have a lot of time to dedicate to these things. But I do have a lot of money."

"And now?" Rosie asked. "What are you going to do now? Your candidate's dead."

He shrugged. "It's a sad situation. He was a very . . ." he paused, looking for the right word. "Principled man. I felt he was the strongest candidate, too. But there are others who can be strong. I'm throwing my support to another candidate."

"Rebecca Gelber?" Rosie guessed.

He shook his head, and offered Rosie more brandy. She declined. She still had some, anyway.

"No, not Rebecca Gelber. Don't misunderstand, I think she's a very capable woman. But—" I could feel Rosie tensing beside me. She guessed what was coming. "Well, it doesn't seem to me to be politically smart to back a woman as our first candidate for governor. Running as an independent on an untried platform— it would simply be another strike against her. I'm sure you can understand that?" He was playing to Rosie, who was not a friendly audience.

"I understand it very well," she said.

"Who then?" I asked.

"Philip Werner is the only viable candidate."

I guess my face went blank.

"You look surprised, Jake," Maddux said.

"I think maybe you could do better," I said diplomatically. He laughed, almost silently. A smile with heavy breathing.

I decided to get off the subject of how he used his money for the time being. It was depressing me. "We heard that you didn't think an investigation into Richmond's death was a good idea. Why's that?"

He looked surprised. "Where did you hear that?"

"Pam. She said Noel Chandler told her that you didn't think much of the idea of hiring us."

He looked enlightened. "Yes, I suppose I did say that."

"Well, why?" Rosie wanted to know. "Did you think he killed himself?"

"Yes. It certainly looked like suicide to me."

"You thought Joe Richmond would actually have killed himself? Why?"

"I don't know why. Possibly the pressure of the campaign got to him. He wasn't handling it all as well as I hoped he would."

"Could you elaborate on that?" I asked.

"No, I don't think so. It's just that he was seeming stressed. Apparently his marriage wasn't good, so perhaps he didn't have the kind of emotional support a man needs to see him through. I don't know. I didn't know that much about the man personally. That's really all I can say about it."

"What's your connection with Noel?" Rosie asked. "Why would he speak for you?"

"My connection, as you put it, was only that he was one of Joe's campaign managers. We talked from time to time. I suppose he asked me what I thought about hiring investigators and I told him. I don't remember. Would you like more?" He gestured toward the decanter. Rosie said no, thanks.

I hit him from still another side. "The morning Joe died, there was a meeting of your PAC in San Francisco. You weren't there. Why was that?"

He smiled slightly, but he was annoyed. "I don't attend every meeting. I was busy elsewhere."

"I see. Where?"

"Actually, as I recall, I started that morning with a strategy talk with Chandler. He had been talking to Ron Lewis and wanted to run some ideas past me. We must have met for at least two hours."

"From when to when?"

"I can't be exact, but I would say from ten to noon or shortly thereafter."

Pam had left her house at ten to go to her meeting. Richmond had not been there at the time. When she'd come back at 12:30, she had found him dead. He had not been dead for more than a couple of hours, according to Hal's connections at the DA's office.

"And what did you do at noon or shortly thereafter?"

"I had a lunch meeting with a financial adviser. I suppose you want to check that?" I didn't, particularly, because the timing was too tight. But I took down the guy's name and number anyway.

"What about Tuesday the fourteenth? Evening?"

He went stiffly to his desk, thumbed through a desk calendar, and gave us the name of a business associate.

"There's one more thing we wanted to ask you about," Rosie said.

He sighed patiently and smiled at her.

"We got a strange phone call last night. A tipster. Someone who said there was a plot within the party to blow up a chemical plant. Right before the election. A faked accident, a disaster, to win votes, to give more power to the Vivo candidate, more support to Vivo as a party."

He had turned even paler than normal for just a second as she spoke. He looked truly horrified.

"That's impossible. A tipster? A maniac. Someone out to destroy . . . you're fabricating it."

"No. But don't you think a disaster like that, a Bhopal right here at home, would do a lot for the Vivo cause? A smallish disaster, justified by the end it would result in—enough power to save the whole planet?"

He stared at her. "I do not. And I think anyone who does think so is very dangerous. In fact, I think anyone who even mentions such a thing is dangerous."

"I'm not dangerous," she said. "I'm a detective."

"And I suppose you said that to watch my reaction? Am I some kind of suspect? Or are you just trying to stir things up? I thought you were a supporter of Vivo."

"I am," she said. "But at this point, we really don't have any idea why someone killed Joe Richmond."

"Yes. I understand that. But I don't think wild flights of imagination are going to solve that problem."

I decided to step in on the argument. "Does Werner know yet that you're going to back his campaign?"

"I talked to him this morning. Why?" He was not as friendly as he'd been at the beginning of our conversation. Now he was wanting to know why we were asking him things. I didn't answer him.

"Just wondering."

"I hope that's all," he said, looking at his watch. "I'm expecting some business calls."

"That's all for now," I said amiably. Rosie and I stood. He stood. We each shook his hand. We told him we would find our own way to the door. He escorted us anyway.

— 24 —

AS we drove to the central Berkeley address Rosie
had gotten for Noel Chandler, I was remembering
my earlier impressions of him, first at the speech and
later at the benefit. I remembered him hopping up on
the stage to introduce Richmond. A graduate student,
I'd thought. Then, at the benefit, when he'd bitched
at Pam about the band, I'd thought of him as a
slightly over-the-hill graduate student, probably in his
thirties. Maybe even a professional student. I hadn't
liked the way he'd talked to Pam. I hadn't liked his
attitude. I reflected that, considering how much I
liked the idea of this group, some of its members
could be downright irritating.

Chandler lived near the UC Berkeley campus, a few
blocks west of Telegraph near Dwight. The building
was an old shingled duplex, painted brown, with a
ratty-looking climbing rose clawing at the gutters and
some soggy impatiens clumped on either side of the
walk. A poster stuck in a downstairs window de-

manded that I support the struggle in—somewhere or other. The second I see the word *struggle* I tend to stop reading. I like fight. I don't mind revolution, although I prefer rebellion. But struggle. Jesus. It's a word used by the kind of jerk who can say People's Tribunal without laughing and who puts an exclamation mark, like an upraised fist, after every sentence he writes.

I checked my watch. We were a few minutes late.

Chandler's name was neatly printed beside one of the buttons. I pressed it. I heard nothing, but a second later a buzzer invited us to push open the downstairs door. We did that, and then we paused in the entry hall, waiting to get further encouragement and maybe some directions.

"Cassandra?" A voice called from above.

"No. Rosie Vicente and Jake Samson." I led the way up the stairs. Chandler's face appeared above me, hanging over a railing.

"I was expecting Cassandra," he complained. "You're late."

"But she's not here yet, so you can talk to us alone anyway." By the time I'd finished the clever stuff, I was up on the second floor, face to face with him. Rosie drew even with me. I smiled. His mouth twitched in a poor imitation. He gestured toward an open door and marched in ahead of us.

"I've got a dinner date, so I don't have a lot of time. What do you two need?"

"A beer would be nice," I said. "If you have one." I was still a little weary from our confrontation with Carl Maddux.

He laughed tentatively, shrugged, shook his head. I waited to see what else he would do. He left the room.

We sat down and waited. I looked around. A very tidy place. Unlike his downstairs neighbor, Chandler didn't have any posters in his windows. A few inoffensive nature prints—and one very nice poster-photo of some desolate spot in Wyoming—on one pristine white wall over a low bookcase that held what looked like pretty good stereo equipment, a couple dozen records, a box of tapes, and a lot of hardcover books. Textbooks. I could make out a few of the titles from across the room. History. There was another bookcase on the wall beside the entry door, with more hardcovers, a lot of paperbacks, and a trendy ceramic lamp on the top shelf. The floor was fir, sanded and finished and without dust bunnies. One large ficus stood on a square table—a black plastic box that also held a black phone—and there was a black leather couch, the brown corduroy chair I was sitting in, and a director's chair with red canvas. Except for the white shaggy rug this furniture surrounded, that was all there was. A door in the wall opposite the one through which my host had gone led, I guessed, to a bedroom. The telephone rang.

Chandler reappeared, handing us each a cheap beer. He had one for himself, too. He put his down and dashed into the bedroom. The phone stopped ringing. I heard the muffled sound of his voice, an "Okay, bye." Then he returned and sat down in the director's chair.

"Nice print," I said, nodding toward "Wyoming."

"Thanks. My home state."

"And now," I said cordially, "you're a graduate student at Berkeley. History?" I gestured toward the shelf of textbooks.

"Where did you get the idea I was a graduate student?" He looked puzzled.

That stopped me for a minute. Hadn't someone told me that? Maybe not. "I thought I heard that you were." I glanced questioningly at Rosie, who looked amused.

"Not from me," she said.

Chandler, too, smiled at my silliness. "Not for years. I'm a social worker. City of Berkeley."

Well, it was almost the same thing. And I couldn't help it if he looked like a graduate student. That was his fault. "Fun," I said. "But actually, that's not what we came to talk to you about."

He tried to keep smiling, but it didn't work. "Right. What's on your mind?"

"Joe Richmond's death. How to get at what really happened. You're one of the people who knew him best. What do you think?"

He shrugged. "Does anyone really know anyone else?"

"You knew him better than I did, better than Rosie did."

"Not better than Pam."

I let that go. "Why would someone kill him? Who would want him out of the way? Who had something to gain? Or did he kill himself?"

He folded his hands neatly in his lap. "Why are you asking me that? How could I know? Sometimes I think I don't know anything."

I glanced toward the bookshelf with all the textbooks. Sure enough, I spotted, in among the histories, several philosophy books. We were going to have to be more concrete in our questioning.

"You didn't think we should investigate," Rosie said. "Why's that?"

"I suppose Pam told you that?" He looked annoyed. Neither of us answered him. He shrugged, his hands still folded in his lap. "I was concerned about the party. Adverse publicity. Private eyes running around . . ." He raised his eyebrows in a semi-apologetic fashion.

"We heard," Rosie persisted, "that you said Maddux didn't want an investigation."

"He mentioned it to me." There was sweat on Chandler's forehead. He didn't wipe it off.

"You and Maddux seem pretty close," Rosie said.

"I don't know what you mean by that, Rosie. We've talked fund-raising a few times. He was important to the campaign." Chandler unfolded his hands, reached for his beer can on the coffee table, took a swallow, and continued to hold the can in both hands.

"Maddux is supporting Werner now," Rosie said. "What do you think of that?"

He frowned, but he looked more relaxed. Safer ground?

"That seems like a reasonable next step. For the sake of the party."

"You haven't really been with the party very long, have you Noel?"

He looked at her resentfully. "There hasn't been a party for very long, but if you mean did I move over to Vivo from the Greens recently, that's true. Just before Joe decided to run for governor, I was thinking about making the move. It was a hard decision. Some of us never made it at all. Some of us made it halfway, like Carney." He looked disgusted.

"Why was it so hard?" I asked. "Vivo stands for the

same things the Greens stand for—peace, justice, ecology—"

"Feminism," Rosie added.

"I don't know how much you understand about our party, Jake. Certainly, our roots are in the Greens. And like the Greens, our people come from a number of different groups . . ."

I nodded. "I've got that part."

He frowned again. Something about my attitude, I guessed. "But Vivo was started by people who were sure they wanted to move faster—Rebecca, Joe, Phil Werner, lots of people. And it took me a while to decide that was okay, was even a good idea. I was still clinging to the idea that we should stay at a grassroots level, keep a low political profile."

"Greens have been winning parliamentary seats in Europe for years now," I said. "How is that keeping a low profile?"

"It's different there. The system is different. Parliamentary government means proportional representation. If you get 10 percent of the vote, you get 10 percent of the seats. Not like here. Here, 10 percent of the votes, 20, means nothing. You get nothing. You can't get anywhere without a broad base of support. You either win or you lose. Maybe that's what finally convinced me. The Greens were using a European model, and that can't work in the United States. If we want to change things—we have to change them. Now." He wasn't sweating anymore. He looked much happier, just talking politics. I thought I'd keep him happy for a while longer, before going back to some hard questions. Relax, then attack.

"Yeah, but didn't I read a while ago that the Greens had a national conference somewhere back East, and then wasn't there some kind of regional thing, here, just last spring? Looks to me like they're trying to get bigger, more national."

He nodded. "They are. They're even planning a platform conference, and maybe by 1990, a founding convention."

"So, there you are," I said, spreading my hands.

"I said 1990! Maybe! Before they even have a convention. Not enough drive, not enough unity or certainty. They have dances to raise money." He shook his head.

"You had a benefit," I said.

"That was to get people involved. It wasn't serious fund-raising." So much for my hundred bucks, I thought. "We've paid more attention to the practical aspects of politics. And we're having a convention next month. With Joe, we had a strong candidate. That was important, too."

"And you think Werner can take his place?" Rosie sounded disdainful.

"Yes."

"Didn't Joe ever tell you he suspected Werner of making plans to bolt the party, take his influence and his supporters and go for more power in a bigger pond? So to speak?"

"Joe didn't tell me," Noel said smugly, "because I told him. I told him that I had heard Werner was hoping to get endorsed and then defect, taking everything with him, convincing people we would be able to get real power within the Democratic party. That's what I heard, and that's what I told Joe."

"Where did you hear it?" I wanted to know.

"Carney. James X. Carney. He told me Werner

tried to get him to go along with the idea. And I believed him. But it was a lie."

"How do you know that?" I asked.

"Carney was just spreading confusion. Trying to get the legitimate candidates squabbling over nonsense, wasting their resources."

"How do you know that?" I asked again.

"Maddux looked into it."

He said the words with great finality and conviction.

"I got a funny kind of phone call last night." I took a long, easy drink of that crummy beer, watching his face. It was blank. He finished his beer and set the can carefully down on the coffee table. "Someone warning us about a plan to create an ecological disaster."

His eyes clamped onto mine. He was sweating again.

"What? What did they say?"

"They—actually, I think it was a woman—said that someone in the party is planning to create a disaster, like Bhopal, only in California somewhere. Sabotage of a chemical plant, made to look like an accident. To win votes. Maybe bad enough to scare people into electing a Vivo for governor."

"That's ridiculous. Ridiculous. No one would do that." His hands were grasping the skinny little wooden arms of his chair. He was still looking hard at me, horrified, defiant, angry. "It must have been the killer, trying to deflect you from himself. It's a lie. Maybe you've forgotten that James X. Carney doesn't want us to back a candidate. Maybe you ought to ask him some questions."

"We plan to, but we have a couple more for you,"

Rosie said. "Like where were you the morning Joe Richmond was killed?"

"I was meeting with Carl Maddux from ten to just after noon." He said it quickly. He had been ready.

"And where were you the night of Joe's funeral?"

He looked surprised. He wasn't ready for that. "What do you mean? What happened?"

"Where were you? Who were you with?"

"Gee, I don't exactly remember—there were meetings that day and the next. Everybody was meeting with everyone else. I'd have to think about it. That evening? I can't remember. A meeting, I think. Or maybe I was with Cassandra."

"We'd appreciate it if you'd figure it out," I said. "How could you spend Tuesday and Wednesday in meetings? You have a job, don't you?"

"I took some vacation time. The future of the party was more important."

The doorbell rang. He jumped up, moved quickly to the entry door, and pushed the buzzer. He walked out into the hall.

"Cassandra?" I heard an answering call from below. I jumped up, too, and joined him in the hall, standing with him as he greeted her and ushered her in. "Are you feeling better?" he asked her. She nodded. She said hello politely, first to me and then to Rosie.

"Cassandra," he said. "These people want to know where I was the day of Joe's funeral in Minneapolis."

"You were at a meeting." She looked skittish.

"Tuesday night?" I asked.

"I don't know about Tuesday night. We were both at big meetings Tuesday morning and Wednesday afternoon."

I remembered Pam mentioning those meetings.

"Look, I'm getting tired of this," Chandler said. "I don't know what I'm supposed to have done Tuesday night, but if I wasn't in a meeting I was home in bed. Now Cassandra and I have dinner reservations, and if you don't mind, we'd like to get there in time to get our table." He walked to the door and opened it.

"We don't mind," Rosie said. "Cassandra, will you be home later?"

"I don't think so." She glanced at Chandler.

I kept listening to Cassandra's voice, trying to match her with the anonymous caller. I couldn't be sure.

"Do you mind?" Chandler shrilled.

Actually, I did. The next morning we were catching a plane to L.A. But then, if she was going to give her boyfriend an alibi she'd have it all clear by the next day anyway.

It was just 6:45 when Noel swept us all out his front door. Our appointment had been for six. I reflected that he hadn't exactly set aside a whole lot of time for us.

—25—

WE had a lunch meeting with Carney; we'd left San Francisco a little earlier than we needed to, and had about an hour to kill after our flight touched down at Los Angeles. We spent it in the airport bar continuing the conversation we'd been having on the plane.

Rosie sipped at her mineral water, scowling at the twist of lime. She tossed it into the drink.

"You still don't know who the caller was?"

She'd asked me the same question at least three times. I shook my head again.

"But the person who called talked a lot," she complained.

"Yeah, that's true. For an anonymous tipster, anyway. But he or she was whispering. I'm not even sure it was a woman. It could have been Cassandra. Maybe. Something in the speech pattern. I don't know. How well do you know Gerda and Cassandra, anyway?"

"Cassandra, not well. I know Gerda better. I like her. If there is some kind of plot in the works, she wouldn't be involved in it. And she certainly wouldn't be involved in anonymous spook stuff."

"No," I agreed. "She's very forthright. To say the least."

"Could it have been Rebecca?"

I shrugged. "I don't think so."

"Maddux bothers me a lot." We'd followed up on his lunch meeting the day of Richmond's death, and on his appointment with a "business associate" the night of the fourteenth. Both checked out. But, of course, his only alibi for the actual hours during which Richmond was killed was Noel Chandler.

"Me too," I agreed. "He's off, somehow. But if you stop to think about it, he's no more unlikeable than Bruce Gelber."

She laughed. We did a little more pawing over the suspects, then went to pick up our rented car. The outside air was warmer than it had been at home, the sun hot.

From the airport, we found La Cienega and headed toward Beverly Hills. The air wasn't much browner than it had been in Oakland that morning. We turned right on Wilshire, to Fairfax. It was only a couple of blocks farther to the restaurant where James X. Carney had asked us to meet him.

The place was called the Chicago Kosher-style Deli. If they'd really been kosher, they wouldn't have been open on a Saturday. But they didn't have to be religious to have great food. It is very hard to find good, really good, Jewish deli in Northern California. Great Italian deli, that's easy. Great gourmet restaurants. Great ethnic food of nearly all varieties except my artery-clogging own. The big problem seems to be the corned beef. This has probably saved my life, but sometimes I resent it.

We stepped inside the door. Nice enough, maybe a little glitzy for my taste in delis. All done in art deco pastels, like it was nouvelle cuisine. But someone had gone to some trouble to steal or have copied a street sign that said Howard St., an avenue of tender memory. Other tender memories were stirred by the smells. A symphony with corned beef brass and roast chicken cellos. Cymbals of horseradish.

I looked around and saw a stocky red-haired man standing up at a booth and looking at us inquiringly. Rosie saw him, too. We walked toward him.

"Carney?"

"That's right." He grinned and stuck out his hand. "Sit down, Jake, Rosie. I think you'll like this place."

"I think I'll love it," I said, sitting. "But I don't remember telling you I'm from Chicago."

He burst out laughing. "You didn't. I'm from Chicago. I didn't live out in Rogers Park, but I had some buddies who did. I just figured a guy named Jake Samson would probably appreciate the food." He smiled at Rosie. "And a woman named Vicente wouldn't be a stranger to it. Want a beer?"

I nodded and smiled back at him. "What I want to know is why the hell you're *not* running for governor."

James X. Carney, it turned out, was about my age and had grown up in Mayor Daley's neighborhood. He had a brother who was a priest and a sister with five kids. He knew more about political patronage than any ten guys who grew up somewhere else. We reminisced about Daley's ward heelers, recalling how many of them were fat, balding men who looked just

like the mayor. We talked about the neighborhood re-
volts in the late sixties and early seventies, culminating
in the '72 Democratic Convention where the machine
showed it was beginning to fail, and the mayor with it.
I don't remember when Richard Daley died, but it
wasn't many years after that. We drank beer and remembered Daley's Chicago, not something you can
ever forget, and Rosie, who grew up in Napa among
the grapevines and was just a kid in 1968, smiled at us
and listened patiently.

I ordered flanken with potato latkes. He ordered a
corned beef sandwich, potato salad, and extra pickles.
Rosie ordered chopped liver on pumpernickel with
pickled green tomatoes. The talk of Chicago dribbled
off. The food came. I decided it was time to maneu-
ver the conversation in a more personal direction.

"So," I said, in a brief interval between mouthfuls,
"you grew up with politics and you were so impressed
you decided to run for governor?"

"You forget," he said, smiling a smile that delayed a
bite of kosher dill, "I'm only trying to get endorsed. I
sure as hell don't want to run."

"Right," I conceded. "You were so impressed with
Chicago politics that you decided to have a party and
not show up."

He shrugged. "The problem is, it's not a party. Not
yet anyway." He finished the pickle. "Let's put it this
way, Jake. I believe Vivo's got a lot of the right answers. But what you have to understand is that the
power in this country is already taken by the two major parties and a few monied special-interest groups.
They make up the government. And even a government that's more or less representative only really
cares about the people it represents—the ones who

can keep them in or toss them out. They care about the people who make the most noise and have the power to back up their noise. So what that amounts to is they care about some people. They don't give a shit about the rest. Not the rest of the people, not the air or the water or the animals. Certainly not about anything that can't yell and can't vote."

He paused. He'd forgotten his sandwich. "And there are still a lot of people on the other side, who see us as nuts and extremists. You think some guy who makes his living, supports his family, working in a refinery, is going to admit that refinery will give his own kid cancer? People have an infinite capacity for taking the short view, painting the scenery green, letting tomorrow, and the planet, take care of itself. Our own planet, for Christ's sake. It's the single most incomprehensible stupidity in a long history of human stupidity, the worst cruelty, the worst sacrilege, the most vicious crime. It's mass suicide and it's mass murder. Richard Daley was a piker. All he did was toss green dye in the Chicago River every Saint Patrick's Day. We got bigger and better now." Carney took a deep breath and ordered another beer.

"Do you hear me arguing with you, Carney?" I said, polishing off the last of the latkes, heavily slathered with death-dealing sour cream. "Don't give me a campaign speech. If you're so goddamn serious about all this, why don't you run for governor and actually run? And change the government?" Big talk, I thought. No action.

He had picked up his sandwich and was chewing again.

"Because," he replied, swallowing, "it doesn't work that way. It's stupid and precipitous and I think it will set us back. We need to change the government, but we need to get stronger first. We need to look like we're for real, and the way to do that is concentrate our energy on becoming a qualified political party, complete with primary ballot. Then we need to concentrate on putting people in the state legislature and then in Congress. We need to be the ones who yell the loudest and pack the most votes. Then we can run a gubernatorial candidate and maybe even think about winning. Now? We're just going to look silly. Just another bunch of goofs endorsing an independent who's going nowhere."

"It's good practice," Rosie said stubbornly.

The wide, lumpy face nodded at her seriously. "Okay, but tell me where you stand. Would you vote for a Vivo candidate for governor? This year?"

"Yes. I would. If it was the right candidate."

"And you, Jake?" His pale blue eyes studied me.

"I'd really have to think about it, Carney. I'd hate like hell to see some asshole elected because the rational people were split."

"Which is another consideration," he said, nodding.

We were all silent for a while, eating, thinking.

"At the same time," I said. "I always thought that was a bullshit reason not to support a third party or an independent."

"There's that as well." He was grinning again.

"Fact is, I hate politics. I don't talk politics. I don't commit myself to politics. I'm investigating Joe Richmond's death at the request of his people, and I don't believe he killed himself. Do you?"

He laughed at me, shaking his head. We finished eating. The place was crowded, all the tables and booths full, and there were people waiting. Carney grabbed the check.

"About Joe," he said. "I don't know. I wasn't there. How long are you two in town for?"

"As long as it takes. We can go back any time today."

"I got an hour, hour and a half to spare. Want to go have some beers somewhere? If you insist, we can talk about Joe Richmond. But we could do something else at the same time."

Rosie said she thought that sounded good. He paid for the lunch, Rosie left the tip, and we went outside, where he led us to a new red Supra. Sunroof. Elaborate stereo with four speakers. White leather interior. He slid behind the wheel. He grinned like a kid.

"Great car," I said. "Did it really come with a white leather interior?"

"Hell no. Came with black, of all the stupid colors for a warm climate. I had this done. You got a car?" I nodded. "Great. Go get it and follow me. Then I won't have to bring you back here and you'll be closer to the airport. You know Venice?"

Both of us admitted we'd been there a couple of times.

We followed the red flash west to about a block from the beach. He pulled up into the front yard of a two-story redwood-and-glass beauty that looked newly renovated. I could hear someone hammering inside. The second story had to have a view of the ocean. He waved at us to pull our car in with his. There was no place to park on the street.

"My house," he said proudly. "I love it as much as I love this car."

"How do you reconcile a love of cars with protection of the environment?" Rosie wanted to know.

"Not easily," he said. "I also eat meat sometimes. I'm not perfect. I'm not a saint." He began walking toward the beach. "I'd ask you in, but they're Sheetrocking. It's a mess."

"Nice piece of real estate," I said.

He laughed. "Well, real estate's my business."

"You like living in L.A.?" Rosie asked. Rosie is a true provincial Northern Californian. It's the only place on earth. I think it's one of the few places on earth, but I like Los Angeles, too, and anywhere on the West Coast is fine with me.

"Yeah," Carney said. "I do. It's a three-ring circus and everything's too far from everything else and the air is bad sometimes. But the air's bad everywhere else now, too, and I like all the ways you can live here. My life's here. My wife has a life here. My kids. I've even got a granddaughter, newborn."

Carney took us to a café with some tables out in front so we could watch the show on the beach and along the wide walk. A guy was standing ankle-deep in soft sand working out with barbells. He was huge, muscles bulging and writhing all over his body. I wondered how fast he could move, wondered what he was like in a fight. Decided his boyfriend probably didn't want him fighting. Our drinks came. Crowds of people were strolling past, rolling past, running past, masses of beautiful and not-so-beautiful bodies played in the sand.

"I guess you like living in a busy neighborhood, too, huh?" Rosie said. She was laughing at a human pyramid forming out near the water.

"Actually, I do," Carney said, smiling. "We used to live up in the hills. Pretty. But I got an itch for, I don't know. City?" He shook his head. "I guess I like walking around here."

"So you really don't have any ideas about Richmond's death?" I got back to business.

"I didn't know him very well."

"You must have some ideas, though," Rosie said.

"Must I now? Well, maybe I must. Did you ever meet the man?"

We told him about the times we'd been around Joe Richmond.

"And what did you think of him?"

"I thought he was a star." I said. "Amazing charisma. Kennedy-like. And I liked him. He was too good-looking, maybe, and he came across like some kind of superman or demigod, but I liked him."

"He wasn't my favorite candidate," Rosie added. "But I thought he was a good one."

Carney nodded thoughtfully. "Yeah. I felt the same way. I liked him. But I don't know if I really trusted him as a candidate for high office. I don't know how much of him was real. I don't know if maybe he wasn't a little too rarefied, a little too perfect. When I was a kid I had a political hero for a while. Adlai Stevenson. But the man really wasn't suited for the rough and tumble, the down and dirty of real-life politics. Stevenson, I mean. Too rarefied. Only difference between him and Richmond, Stevenson showed it. I met him once, at a neighborhood rally. I pushed my way up to the front and grabbed his hand to shake. The guy looked horrified."

"You think Richmond was too delicate? You think maybe he wasn't too stable under all that star shine?"

"Could be."

"Are you saying you think he could have killed himself?" Rosie was ready and waiting. Now we were going to start getting down to it.

"I don't know. I guess I'm saying a guy like that could have a—well, an episode of some kind, maybe over something personal. You're the investigator, you tell me. You got anything that makes it look like murder?"

Rosie shrugged. "Nothing we're ready to talk about."

He nodded slowly at her. "I understand. I guess I could be a suspect. I was an opponent, after all. Interesting idea. Because I wanted to win or because— what, I didn't want us to field an actual candidate and I'm a fanatic? Well, why not?"

"That's right," Rosie said, smiling to soften her words. "Why not?"

A man and woman, both dressed in bikinis covered by thin overshirts, roller-skated by and skidded to a stop just past us, looking at the human pyramid.

"You didn't go to his funeral. Why was that?"

"I was busy, and I'm not a hypocrite."

Rosie again: "You didn't think there should be an investigation."

"I was actually kind of neutral. Unenthusiastic, maybe."

"So, you were busy the day of his funeral?" I tried to mix just the right amount of disapproval with the suspicion. "Doing what?"

"Visiting my new granddaughter in the hospital." He smiled a leprechaun smile.

"And that night?"

"Having a party celebrating my granddaughter, what else?"

"What about the day he died?" Rosie shot back at him.

"That would have been on the Sunday . . . sorry, I guess you've got me. I was out walking. Alone."

"I got a phone tip that someone in the party is planning an ecological disaster right before the election," I said. "To get votes for Vivo."

He turned gray. "Are you shitting me?"

"No."

"Who was it? Who called you?"

"I don't know."

"What did they say?"

I told him.

He shook his head. "Someone's playing games with you."

"Isn't it possible?" Rosie asked. "Possible that there's someone in the party who would do that?"

"Oh, I suppose it's possible," he admitted. "But not for just any madman. You'd have to have money, you'd have to be able to get to people. And you'd have to be getting something out of it."

"And who does that describe?" Rosie asked.

"It used to describe Joe Richmond."

"Would it describe someone who was now going to get the backing Richmond had?"

He rubbed his eyes and looked at her. "It could."

The bikini-clad man squatted. His girlfriend climbed onto his back, skates and all. They were laughing hysterically. He skated off, wobbling, carrying her on his shoulders.

"Could it describe Philip Werner?" I asked.

"Really? That's what's going on now? That son of a bitch. Sure, it could describe him."

"I guess you don't like him."

"Not much, no."

"Because he was planning to defect if he got Vivo's backing? Sell his support base to a major party? His status? Isn't that what you told Noel Chandler?"

"That's right. He figured the governorship was unreachable in any case—he might as well get a place in a real power structure." He sighed, drank, shook his head. "If he's got enough of Richmond's people, he'll get the endorsement."

"Well, he could still follow up on his original plan," Rosie said.

Carney looked baleful. "Sure, unless he thinks he's come up with a way to actually win the election."

That did sum things up in a nutshell, I had to admit. We all sat there looking at each other for a while, drinking our cold drinks, thinking cold thoughts.

"Where did you hear that Werner was going to bolt the party?" Rosie asked.

"One of his own campaign people. He was feeling me out—I'm a bit of a wild card in this game, after all. I didn't want us to have a candidate, see. And, as it turned out, Werner wasn't going to be a candidate if he won, anymore than I was. So his people were sort of interested to know what I was 'really planning.' If I could see my way clear to support him and promise the support of my people if he got the endorsement. They wanted a deal. They didn't exactly admit he was going to take his supporters and go somewhere else, but that was the implication. The clear implication. They thought maybe I could go along with that, if I got a piece of what they thought they'd get. I couldn't. Dishonest piece of shit."

"But why would you tell that to Noel Chandler, of all people?" Rosie asked.

"Because he was sleazing around me in the same kind of way. Trying to get me to throw my support to Richmond. I laughed at him. Told him I'd gotten a better offer."

Again, we were all quiet for a moment.

"Maybe," he continued, "I'd better get a little more serious about this governor thing. I've been thinking about it anyway, since Joe died. I could have lived with him as a candidate. But not Werner. It didn't matter so much when I thought he wouldn't run anyway. But if what you say is actually true, and he's got some idea he can actually win, he has to be stopped. If it's true. Hell, even if it isn't. Dishonest piece of shit. Maybe I need to drop out of the thing, turn my support over to Rebecca. Before they get a chance to blow up Bakersfield or merge with the Democrats or whatever they plan to do. They. Werner. What a mess."

"Why the hell don't you just run for real?" I wanted to know. "Go after the endorsement? I mean aside from all those terrific political reasons you gave us a while ago."

"Because I don't want the damned thing, that's why."

I believed him. He didn't want the damned thing.

"Tell me this," I said. "Did Rebecca know you might swing over to her if Joe was out of it?"

He nodded. "As a matter of fact she did. It's something we discussed once. And she brought it up again, after he died."

When Carney said good-bye to us at our car, I took his arm, made him look me in the eye.

"James X.," I said. "Don't go off half-cocked on any of this. Give us a few more days. Bakersfield isn't going to get blown up yet. Not for months. Sit on it until you hear from us, okay?"

"You've got a week," he said. "No more."

— 26 —

MOSTLY, Sacramento is a place I pass through on my way to the Sierra, a not-quite-halfway mark in the trek to Tahoe. Close enough to the Bay Area so some people actually commute, and so government people with nothing better to do can take their nightlife where no one's paying attention.

Werner knew we were coming. The night before, I'd called Pam to confirm what she'd learned earlier in the week. He was spending the weekend at his home base. Then I'd called him at home to make an appointment. I didn't say anything about his skip in Minneapolis; neither did he.

Rosie and I spent the night in L.A. and flew to Sacramento first thing Sunday morning.

I had thought about not calling first, about sneaking up on him. But that would have given him an excuse to disappear. If he walked out on me again, with an actual commitment to meet, I swore I'd find some way to skewer the bastard.

We were supposed to meet him at his law office at 10:00 A.M. It was easy to find. A five-story red brick office building downtown, within sight of the waffle dome of the capitol building. When we got to his office building it was closed, but the guard checked us off his list, alerted Werner, and sent us upstairs.

Werner, true to my first impression of him, was dressed in those dumb-looking clothes people wear for hiking. Shorts, camouflage shirt, clunky boots, clunky socks. He looked ten years younger than he'd looked in a suit at the funeral. He was already standing when we walked in, smiled pleasantly, shook hands, and asked us to sit down.

"I came in for an hour just to talk to you. Then I have to take off." He gestured vaguely at his hiking gear. "Coffee?" We accepted. He poured us some from a machine near the window, and got our orders for milk and sugar. Real milk, from a tiny refrigerator. He sat back down.

"I'm surprised you're actually here," I said, smiling.

He smiled back. "Look, Samson, I'm sorry if you think I was trying to avoid you in Minneapolis. I wasn't. It just worked out that way. I got an urgent message from one of the groups I'm working with—a problem we thought we had another month to work on was moving along too fast. I had to catch the next plane back and, to be honest, I forgot about you." He continued to smile, which did not succeed in making the words friendly.

"And what problem was that, the important one that came up?"

He smiled and shook his head. "A new pesticide. Supposed to solve the selenium runoff problems. We think it may be even more dangerous. There's some big money behind the company, of course." Selenium.

That was the stuff that was poisoning a wildlife refuge somewhere in the state and killing the ducks.

I accepted that for the moment. I looked appraisingly around his expensive-looking office. "Are you doing it for the cause—or for a fee?"

"You know, Jake, you're not exactly charming me."

"I'm not trying to."

He turned to Rosie. "Is he always this easy to get along with?"

"Always," she said.

He laughed. "Well, good. I'd hate to think I was getting special treatment." He leaned back in his swivel chair and looked at us benevolently. "You didn't travel to Sacramento to insult me. What's up?"

I was having a problem. It would have been easier for me to distrust him if he'd been dressed in a business suit. He looked too much like a real person dressed as he was. I hadn't been able to make him hostile, either.

"There are one or two people who think you're the perfect candidate for murderer of Joe Richmond. We thought we'd ask you about that," I said.

He shook his head. "Sorry, you'll have to draft someone else." He sipped his coffee and put his hiking boots up on his oak desk. "Why me?" He managed to look mildly curious.

Rosie answered. "Because you're second in line for the Vivo endorsement. And whatever support that brings. First, now."

He looked surprised. He was not convincing. "Where'd you get that idea? I'm running strong, yes, but Rebecca's at least as strong. Maybe stronger."

"That's not what everybody else in the party says," she insisted.

He gave her a wry smile. "Who have you talked to?"

"We talked to Maddux," I said. "And Chandler."

"And who else? Ron Lewis? James X. Carney? And Pam Sutherland, what about Pam?" He laughed. "Surely you've heard the famous story that I'm a turncoat? How many votes do you think that's going to win me?"

Damn, I thought. He stole one of our best questions.

"Who do you think started the story?" Rosie asked. "Carney?" He shrugged. "Rebecca Gelber?" A much smaller shrug.

"I think it was started to benefit another candidate, certainly."

"Rebecca doesn't believe the story about you is true," Rosie said. "That's what she told us."

He pursed his lips, a judicious look I thought he probably practiced in front of the mirror. "She's the other candidate. She has to look clean and generous."

That was true, of course.

"Chandler says it was all a lie made up by Carney," I said. "To confuse everyone and make a mess of the convention."

Again, he only shrugged.

"If your supporters can convince people that's true, you'll probably get the endorsement." He gazed out the window, trying not to look bored.

"And we heard something else, too," Rosie said. "Although it wasn't exactly a rumor. More like a tip." She told him about the anonymous phone call.

His reaction was odd. Others we'd told had reacted with shock, fear, even anger. Some of their reactions had seemed somehow exaggerated, as if they were trying to convince us that they were appalled. But Werner was a very cool character. He paled slightly, but showed only a moment's surprise, then, gazing thoughtfully at neither one of us, nodded slightly. He thought for what seemed like a long time.

Then, to me: "Do you believe it?"

"I think it's possible. I don't want to believe it."

"It would be incredibly risky," he said. "One mistake could destroy Vivo as a party and every serious career politician involved in it."

"Not only that," Rosie said sharply, "They'd make a big mess."

"I understand that," he snapped. "I was merely commenting that it's also extremely risky."

He got out of his chair and walked to the window. He stood there, looking out, hands clasped behind his back, flexing his knees. From where I sat, I couldn't tell if he had a view of the capitol dome, or maybe could catch a corner of the governor's mansion. I sighed. Sometimes I miss Jerry Brown.

"Do you two have a line on who might be hatching a plot like that—if there is one?"

"We thought it might be you," I said.

He turned and frowned at me. "I wish you'd get it through your heads I'm not the only Vivo in this race." He sat down again. "Since you seem to be going in the wrong direction on this thing, maybe I'll look into it myself."

"If it's true," I warned, "that could be dangerous."

He laughed, stirred his coffee with his finger, finished it off. "It already is. Was there anything else you wanted to know about?"

I told him we wanted to know where he was when Richmond died, and where he went after Richmond's funeral.

"The day Joe died, I was here in town. I was meeting with some people who are part of a statewide conservation group. We were working on that pesticide crap I was telling you about. And I told you where I went after the funeral. I flew back here for another meeting the next day. Some of the same people."

"I hate to keep sounding suspicious, Phil, but how about you give us their names and numbers, just so we can double-check?"

"No problem, Jake," he said, imitating my ironic friendliness. He consulted a leather-covered address book, and wrote out three names and numbers. "And maybe it would help if I showed you this stuff." He went to an oak file cabinet in the corner, opened it, and pulled out a file labeled "Fielding Agricultural Products." He handed it to me. I looked through the papers, passing them on to Rosie. Correspondence, newspaper clippings, copies of testing information. I read some of it. He was definitely involved in working on the project he described. There was definitely some time pressure involved in it. Other than that, we'd have to talk to the people whose names he'd given us.

"Where were those meetings in Sacramento?" Rosie asked. He gave her the name of a motel. Good move, I thought. A backup check in case some of the people whose names we had weren't telling the truth. Rosie obviously trusted Werner as much as I did.

We said good-bye, wished him a pleasant hike, or whatever it was he was planning on doing in his hiking clothes, and left. The sky was clouding up. Looked like a late-season rain was coming, probably the last of the year. We climbed into our rental car and prepared for a damp Sunday in the metropolis of the central valley, checking up on Philip Werner. I hoped his pretty hiking clothes got wet.

191

——27——

WE didn't reach everyone on our list, but close enough. We even found a motel employee who remembered the meetings, and Werner was on the books—he'd reserved and paid for the meeting rooms. It wasn't until late evening that we finished, so we stayed over and drove home the next morning.

We had agreed, by this time, on a couple of possible solutions, and were planning return visits with several people in the Bay Area. We weren't sure how we could force the issue and knew it would have to be attacked from more than one side, since there was no way to be sure yet who was involved in what. But we were beginning to feel we were coming close.

Rosie went off to pick up Alice from the friend who'd been keeping her and I took care of my own housekeeping. Tigris and Euphrates had stayed home, fed by a neighbor who had also carried my mail to the front porch and stuck it under a long-unoccupied flowerpot. The cats were waiting in the kitchen, with numerous complaints. I fed them, told them they were gorgeous, dropped my suitcase on the bed, and glanced through my mail. My dentist was concerned that I was neglecting my dental health and urged me to call for an appointment soon. A couple of bills. I checked my answering machine for messages.

Marietta had called.

"Hello, Jake. This is Marietta Marple—just a joke, she was old. Marietta Richmond, of course. I wanted you to know that I have continued to be hot on the trail of my daughter-in-law. Actually, she's my former daughter-in-law now, isn't she? That, at least, is a relief.

"I stole Emily's little diary, or journal, or whatever it is. I went to visit her to extend my mutual grief and I stole it. I don't think she had anything to do with killing my son. There's nothing in that book but poetry. Not a word about murder, although with poetry it's hard to tell, isn't it?

"Anyway, I can't think of anyone else in the family who could have done it and Emily's gone back to L.A. I need your advice, dear. Please call and set me moving again. Bye."

Set her moving again? That was the last thing I wanted to do.

The second message was from Gerda.

"This is Gerda Steiner. This is Saturday afternoon. I am calling because I think something is funny with Cassandra. She will not talk to me. I think you must talk with her again."

The third message was from Cassandra.

"Hello. This is Cassandra calling. It's Monday

morning. I don't know why I'm calling you, but I don't know where else to go. Please call me back."

Hearing her on the phone helped. It was a habit of speech, her way of saying "I don't know," with strong emphasis on the "know." Something small, that stuck in a crevice in my brain. I'd heard her say it when we'd talked to her about Richmond's fling with Gelber. And the anonymous caller had whispered it the same way. I was almost sure.

There was a fourth message, too, this one from Rebecca Gelber.

"Jake, please call, or come over. I'll be home all day and evening—this is Monday. It's very important."

This was still Monday. I tapped out Gerda and Cassandra's number. No answer. No machine. I called Rosie and told her about the messages, about Cassandra's voice. We met in the driveway, jumped into Rosie's pickup, and drove the few blocks to the storefront apartment.

"Gerda's car isn't here," Rosie said. "Or Cassandra's."

I banged on the front door. Nothing. Put my eye to a two-inch gap in the canvas window covering. No one. Rosie had found another gap in the one on the other side. She didn't see anything, either. We went around to the back of the building, and found the outside stairs. The back door had no window. I banged on it. There was a good-sized, uncovered window about two feet from the tiny, railed back porch. I climbed up, one foot on the railing and the other on a narrow ledge that ran just below the window, holding tight to the back door molding and grabbing the window frame, and looked in. A clean kitchen, with two doors leading to two bedrooms just beyond. All very tidy. No immediate sign of any violence. If there were any corpses, they were lying tucked up on a bedroom floor in a corner. I edged my foot backward along the ledge, brought it to the railing, turned, and jumped back down to the porch floor. I looked at Rosie and shrugged.

"Should we break in?" she asked.

I was reluctant. There was no sign of anyone, no cars. Everything pointed to an empty apartment. I looked around. Just down the block, an elderly woman was peeking over her fence, watching us. All we needed at this point was to have to waste time with the cops.

We drove to College Avenue, found a phone booth, and called Gelber.

The husband answered.

"Samson? Good. Rebecca's been trying to reach you. You'd better get over here right now." He hung up. Wonderful. I loved the guy.

We headed north to Benicia.

— *28*—

REBECCA Gelber looked harassed and confused. Her hair wasn't perfect. She almost looked her age.

"Jake, Rosie, I'm glad you're here." She waved us in. "My husband and I have been trying to have dinner for three hours now. First Cassandra, then Phil. At least you were invited." She sat down heavily in an armchair and waved vaguely at us, indicating we could sit.

I didn't know who to ask her about first. For a second, I just sat there, stunned. "Phil?"

She nodded.

"Start at the beginning," Rosie said. "Please. First Cassandra?"

"Yes. She showed up here looking very nervous. She said she wanted to talk to me about something, but she couldn't seem to get it out. Then she asked if she could stay here for a few hours, maybe overnight. I said she could. I didn't want to press her about why, or what it was she wanted to tell me. She looked so awful. I had her sitting down in the kitchen with us, finally, at dinner. Then the bell rang again. Bruce got up. He came back and told me Phil Werner was here and wanted to talk to me. I was surprised, to say the least. Phil is not an informal man. It must have been soon after that that you called. I heard the phone ring while I was talking to Phil."

"What did he want?" I asked.

"That was very confusing. He was so oblique. He asked me about an anonymous phone call, wanted to know what I knew about one. He was, well, he seemed accusing, as if I knew or had done something, and he acted as if I were keeping some secret from him or telling a secret or some peculiar thing. He wanted me to admit this secret without telling me what it was. He kept asking me, 'Did you make that call?' It was really rather ugly."

Bruce Gelber walked into the room and glared at us. We said hello. He nodded.

Rebecca turned to him. "I was telling them about Phil."

This time, there was no word from Rebecca letting him know we were talking about her business. He was in on it.

"Pretty damned peculiar, too," he snarled. "I went back into the kitchen. Couldn't have been more than a minute later when you called. But I could hear Werner, out here. He sounded threatening. I got off the phone and made short work of that."

"Uh huh," I said. "Maybe even a good thing you did. He left?" They both nodded. "Did he say where he was going, by any chance?" They both shook their heads. "And Cassandra?"

"That was strange, too, Jake," Rebecca said.

"It was," her husband agreed. "No sooner had I told Rebecca that Werner was here, and sat down at the table with Cassandra, when that young woman slipped out the back door. We haven't seen her since. I feel like I'm living in a movie. And most of it on an empty stomach." His beeper went off. "Oh, shit," he said, and left the room. "Never a minute . . ."

I told Rebecca about the anonymous call, the warning that someone was planning a catastrophe. She looked at me as if I'd lost my mind.

"And I think Cassandra made the call," I said.

"And just yesterday," Rosie added, "we were sitting in Werner's office in Sacramento questioning him about it."

"Is it true?"

"I'm beginning to think so," I admitted. "Since asking people about it seems to have stirred things up so much. I'm really afraid it's so."

"But there's time," she said. "If it's not planned until after the convention."

"Right."

"But you'll need to catch Philip."

"Can we use your phone?" Rosie asked.

"Good God, Rosie, of course you can. My phone, my house, my car. Everything but my husband." It was a feeble attempt at a joke, but I could see she was having trouble keeping calm. I didn't blame her.

We called Gerda's number again. This time she answered.

"Gerda," Rosie cried. "We've been looking for Cassandra. She did? Well, stay put. We'll be right there."

She hung up. "Gerda just talked to her. On the phone. She said she was on her way home."

I told Rebecca not to worry, that everything was under control. Positive thinking. Rosie and I drove south again, to Oakland.

Cassandra was not home.

"Didn't you say she was on her way?" I said.

"That is what she said," Gerda answered. "I do not know from where. She did say she might stop off at Noel's apartment first."

Rosie agreed to stay put, in case Cassandra showed up. Or in case someone else showed up.

"No heroics," I said. "If you have to, call the cops."

"Same to you, pal."

I went to Berkeley.

There was a light on in Noel's place, which might or might not mean he was there. I rang the bell. The buzzer sounded. I pushed the door open.

"Who is it?" Noel called out.

"Samson."

"Go away." I kept walking up the stairs. Footsteps. I looked up to see him peering over the railing. He started down, rushing me. He was carrying a suitcase in one hand and his trendy deco ceramic lamp in the other. "Get out of my way, Samson." I didn't. I put myself directly in front of him and braced my legs. He swung the suitcase at my chest, and as my hands went out to protect that part of me he brought the lamp down toward my head. I ducked, going for his midsection. But he had the advantage, two steps above me. His lamp connected with my head before my head connected with his gut. A glancing blow, stunning but not quite a knockout. As I fell down the stairs, I heard a crash and a terrible yell. Someone bumped into me from below and kept going. More yelling. Footsteps thumping up the stairs. Rosie was beside me.

I stood up, swaying, and saw Cassandra, wide-eyed, clutching the splintered frame of the front door, her red hair a tangled, flying mess. "Noel," I croaked to Rosie.

"Gerda went after him."

"Help her." I lurched out the front door. There had to be a back way, and I could imagine Noel outrunning Gerda and escaping down the back stairs to his car. I would die before I let that son of a bitch get away.

He was close to the bottom of the stairs when I got there, just in time to see Gerda, two steps above him, wrap him in a stranglehold. Rosie had just come out the back door. He was kicking and elbowing and thrashing. I grabbed him, yanked him out of Gerda's hands, spun him around and smashed him into the building, which lost a few shingles. Then I hit him, hard, several times. It felt great. Nobody hits me on the head twice and gets away with it. I was only sorry I probably wouldn't get a chance to drown him in his own shower.

—29—

NOEL was more than willing to talk to the police, hoping, I suppose, that talking would help him get away with murder. Or at least get a lighter sentence for it. He probably thought it was a good idea to dump on Maddux before Maddux dumped on him.

He sent the cops to Maddux's Ross house, where they found Werner and Maddux pretending to negotiate. The candidate was looking for information to use to his own advantage; Maddux, alone in the house with Werner, was killing time, after calling Noel, waiting for his boy to arrive and help him get rid of the candidate.

They both tried to have the other arrested. They both got hauled off to the station.

But then, Maddux could have waited forever for Noel. When we'd caught him he'd been on his way out of town.

Cassandra was ready to tell what she knew, too. What she knew was what she'd whispered to me on the phone a few nights before. Well actually, she had left out the part about the information coming from an eavesdropped phone conversation between Chandler and Maddux, and stuck in a reference to Werner, from that same conversation, that proved to be irrelevant.

As for Werner, the cops turned him loose pretty quickly. They had nothing on him. And the first thing he did was call a news conference. He told the assembled scribblers that he had been instrumental in exposing the plot, had been at Maddux's house tracking it down, as a matter of fact. That he had first gotten word over the weekend through anonymous sources and had been determined to prevent the disaster.

He was heartsore, he said, that the good name of the Vivos had been destroyed by the insane acts of a few men. Too often, he said, dangerous people, "the kind of people capable of this ultimate dirty trick," were drawn to good causes and found homes in minor parties and "would-be parties that could never hope to have a real effect, create real change." That was why, he said, he was declaring as a Democrat and was, as a matter of fact, planning to run for the assembly on a conservation platform.

He got big coverage for his little speech, too, because the media believed him and included him in their stories about the "barely averted disaster."

What the hell, Rosie and I couldn't very well stand up there and say, "No! It was us! Unlicensed private detectives! He didn't solve it, we did!"

In fact, when Sergeant Cotter of the Berkeley police department wanted to know what the hell we thought we were doing, anyway, we told him Werner did it.

Cotter, at least, had the sense not to believe that, but he took what credit he could for Chandler's confession and left us alone.

We got home very late that night. I called Pam, woke her up, told her it was over, and said we would meet her the next day and give her a full report. The next morning I called James X. Carney. He was relieved, but kind of quiet about it. Thoughtful. Then I called Marietta Richmond and told her she could stop whatever investigation she was still conducting. She was disappointed, I think, but glad the killer was caught.

After I finished talking to Marietta, I called Lee at her office. I told her how we'd solved the case and said all the bad guys—well, most of them—were in jail. She said that was wonderful.

"Are we still on for tomorrow night?" I asked her.

"I was going to call you about that, actually . . . I don't think so, Jake."

"Why not?" I asked, reasonably. I couldn't yell. My head still hurt from the ceramic lamp.

"Well, I've been thinking about it, that's all. You weren't happy about the idea. You didn't love me enough to make a commitment right away."

"That's not true. I did—do—love you." I had never said that to her; I wasn't sure it was true. "But that has nothing to do with my reluctance to commit to having a child, and my reluctance to go along with extortion." I was getting pissed off at her again.

"Maybe not," she said. "But your reluctance has

something to do with how I feel about you. Let's just forget it. We can still be friends."

I doubted that. The thing was, I had felt pretty involved with her, and I was more than a little upset at the outcome. I went back to bed and lay down, fuming, hurt, trying to decide whether I should dash to Petaluma and try to make it all right again. I didn't think it would work, so I went back to sleep.

Rebecca Gelber invited Rosie and me to the convention, which was held in San Jose. We made plans to drive down with Pam who was, I thought, maybe beginning to see her way clear of grieving for Joe Richmond.

Just before I left the house, bag in hand, my father and stepmother called. Eva wanted to thank me for the birthday flowers. Pa got on the kitchen extension to join the chat.

Neither one of them could get over the fact that I was going to a political convention.

"So what is this party called?" Eva wanted to know.

"Vivo," I said for the fifteenth time.

"And what does it mean, Vivo?"

"'Life.' In Esperanto. They're an ecology party. Terrific people."

"Didn't I hear something about some ecology party was going to blow up California?" My father said. He reads the newspaper every day and remembers almost everything. He remembers it oddly, but he remembers it.

"There were some crazy people, Pa, not the whole party. One man planned it. Not the party."

"So tell me this," Eva said. "This Vivo. They're Democrats?"

Ron Lewis was at the convention, working as some

sort of media consultant for Rebecca Gelber, whose husband had managed to make it to this event. Lewis knew some of the bits and pieces of the story, but wanted all the details. Pam, Rosie and I went out for a long dinner with him the night before the convention opened and went through it with him.

I'd invited James X. Carney, but he seemed to be awfully busy.

The one thing Lewis wanted to know most of all was whether Joe Richmond had any idea of what kind of man he'd gotten involved with.

I reassured him. "He didn't. Not right away. Not until the end, actually."

The night of the benefit, Richmond had confided to Noel that he was feeling worried about the campaign. He wasn't sure, he told him, that he trusted Maddux. The man was forever sidling up to him with suggestions, he said. He felt as if he were selling himself to someone dishonest for an election he couldn't win, as if he'd gotten into something he couldn't get out of without getting out of the race. Noel, of course, was horrified. Everything was planned, and he had already sold himself.

"If Noel had had any sense," I said, "he would have gone to his boss right then and asked him what to do. But he didn't. He tried to talk to Richmond. About what he called 'necessary evils.'"

"Oh, lord," Lewis said.

"Lord, indeed," Rosie agreed. "As nearly as we can figure out, he actually told Richmond that Maddux had a plan that would bring a lot of votes, and said that Richmond should have faith and hang on."

Richmond wanted to know what the plan was. Noel realized he'd gotten himself in a hole, asked Richmond if they could talk about it the next day. Richmond didn't want to wait, but he agreed. The next morning he called Noel and told him to meet him at his East Bay retreat—Pam's house. Pam would be gone. They could talk.

"And meanwhile," I said, "Noel Chandler had gotten his instructions. Meet with him. Fix it. If you can't fix it, kill him. And make it look like he did it himself. I don't know who actually came up with the hanging idea, but Noel, a Wyoming boy, probably felt pretty much at home with a rope."

"Joe must have had no idea about Noel," Pam said. "He must have been sitting in the hot tub when Noel . . ."

"Dropped the rope around his neck and pulled," Lewis murmured. Pam nodded, and excused herself.

"Shit," Lewis said, looking after her.

"She'll be okay," Rosie said.

I continued the story, telling Ron about my little ordeal in Minneapolis.

"That's cute. He could have killed you."

"That wasn't the object, but they wouldn't have minded. They were trying to scare us off."

All they had to do was find out where I was staying. Then Noel could go to his morning meeting, fly to Minneapolis, torture me, and fly back again for his meeting the next day.

I had remembered that Pam, when she'd arrived for the funeral, had said everyone in the organization ·was harassing her, wanting to know when she was going back, where she could be reached. She had specifically mentioned talking to Noel. When I got back to Minneapolis I confirmed it with her—Noel, along with Gerda, had known that the number she gave them was my hotel number.

The anonymous telephone tip, even before I realized who had called, brought in another element. Power. If there was such a plot, it would take money, power and connections to pull it off. The other candidates were still unknown quantities. I didn't think Rebecca Gelber had that kind of stuff going for her, even if I had thought she was capable of such a thing. Richmond had been collecting money and power. Who was next in line? Maddux told us he was switching his support to Werner. The caller had said, "Ask Werner."

Werner was a wild card in the game, but we'd gotten no indication he had any real money or power before he hooked up with Maddux—and the fake accident had been planned before he had access to Maddux's backing.

Pam came back and sat down. Her eyes were red and a little swollen.

"What about Carney?" she asked. "Why not him?"

"A man who knows where to get a good corned beef sandwich," I said, "is not a man of violence." She smiled. "Besides, he didn't have anything to gain, not unless he was a screaming fanatic who wanted to kill off the front-runner so Vivo wouldn't have a candidate. I've lived around the Bay Area long enough to know a screaming fanatic when I see one." She smiled again.

"So you thought Maddux must be the key," Lewis said.

"We thought he might be. And if he was, it was significant that he and Noel alibied each other for the morning of the murder. Noel was obviously in the man's pocket."

"And," Rosie added, "Noel could have been anywhere the night of Richmond's funeral. Cassandra made it clear to us she didn't know where he was that night."

"What about Cassandra?" Lewis asked. "What the hell was she doing? How did she find out about the plot?"

"That is one very suspicious woman," Rosie said. "She had a thing about men being untrustworthy. Noel had been acting pretty peculiar. On Thursday night, when she was at his apartment, his phone rang and he took the call in the bedroom. She was in the living room. He closed the bedroom door to talk. That made her mad. She picked up the living room extension. First she heard a small part of a reference to Werner, then she heard Maddux and Noel talking about the toxic accident."

"I guess they were talking about supporting Werner," Lewis said.

Rosie smiled. "Actually, they were talking about Werner's campaign against Fielding Chemical. Noel thought they should switch the disaster there—I think it's somewhere near L.A.—to Werner's bad guys, to give more weight to Werner's campaign. Maddux told him he was a moron, that everything was already in place for the original plan."

"Anyway, Cassandra freaked out, as we used to say," I added. "She sat around with him for a while, faked illness, and went home. Once she got there, she decided to handle it with an anonymous tip. The next day, when we went to talk to Noel, and she showed up, he asked her if she was feeling better. She could have been sick earlier that day, sure, but he also could have been talking about a problem the night before. Which would work out just fine if she had actually been the caller."

Once we were pretty sure the caller was telling the truth, and once I was pretty sure that the caller was Cassandra, it all fell into place. Why would she be acting weird, not wanting to tell but wanting to tell? Was she involved? Or was she going crazy because her boyfriend was involved?

"And you had to worry about protecting her, too." Pam said.

"That was a problem," I explained. "We didn't know how much danger Cassandra was in. We couldn't both sit around her place with Gerda, waiting for her to show up so we could talk to her. We were worried about her being in danger from three possible sources at that point: Maddux, Noel, even Werner. We really didn't know what the hell Werner was doing in town.

"I went to Noel's and found him trying to take off. Meanwhile, Cassandra showed up at home and told Rosie and Gerda everything she knew. Then they came racing to help me, dragging Cassandra along with them just in case someone came looking for her.

"The other two suspects, however, were nowhere near Berkeley. They were across the Bay, fighting with each other."

"So Werner wasn't really in it, then," Lewis mused.

Rosie shook her head. "No. He was about as clean as a sleazeball can be."

Werner had accepted Maddux's support, and had agreed that in exchange, he would actually run for the governorship. According to Noel, he didn't understand why Maddux thought he'd get a lot of votes in the general election, but he seemed willing to go along for the ride. That kind of attitude was what had attracted Maddux to him in the first place: his earlier plans to scuttle the party and go after personal power—that part had been true—and his willingness to cut a different kind of deal if he could get power that way. A perfect candidate, unlike Joe Richmond. A man who could be bent. A man who wouldn't ask questions, wouldn't get in the way of Maddux's own plans and ambitions.

Lewis ordered a third martini. Pam had stopped drinking half an hour before. I wanted a cigarette, but nobody smokes any more, not even me.

"I saw the story in the paper," Lewis said. "About the arrests they made out in the Central Valley."

"Yeah, thanks to Chandler," I said. He had known enough about the plan, and about Maddux's habits, to send the police looking in the right drawers and strongboxes for the information they needed to get to the people who were actually going to carry out the sabotage. They were caught before word got out about Maddux's arrest.

The target pesticide factory was in Fresno, smack in the middle of California. Some of their chemicals were pretty volatile, and Maddux had a man inside who knew just how to make them blow up "accidentally," while giving himself enough time to catch a flight the hell out of there. Because the explosion would have poisoned the city, and the toxic cloud would have totally contaminated the immediate area for fifty miles around and drifted, like fallout, God knows how far.

— *30* —

THE party had started with four major candidates: Richmond, Carney, Werner and Gelber.

Richmond was dead, Werner was a Democrat, and Carney? Halfway through the first day, it became apparent that Carney wasn't going for the endorsement at all. He was supporting Rebecca, and some of the people in his faction were going along with him.

There were three days of platform hassles before everybody could agree to be dissatisfied. The Vivos did include a wide range of political complexions, and the world-peace and social-ills issues came in for a lot of left-right fights. Both planks, unlike the strong ones on environmental problems, became very generalized in the end, mentioning no specific factions in Central America, no specific interest groups at home. After all, they wanted to become a real party.

On the fourth day, they got down to the candidates. A bunch of latecomers were making noise, but none of them seemed to have much chance of getting enough votes. By then, everyone knew that James X. Carney would make the big speech for Rebecca Gelber.

It was a dandy. He talked about how he had decided there was no more time to waste. He said their first foray into big-time politics had brought them corruption and that corruption had almost destroyed them. They had been through their baptism, he said, their trial by fire. And they were still alive. And to stay alive, now, they had to unite and come out fighting. They had a world to save. They had a candidate who would take their story to the voters. A woman who . . . he brought down the house.

When the voting was over, Gelber had it by a wide margin. In her acceptance speech, she talked about Joe Richmond, and a lot of people cried. Pam did, and I held her.

She talked about the future, and about change, about honor and nonviolence and respect for life. Then, at the end, she announced that James X. Carney had agreed to serve as her campaign manager.

The two of them ran one hell of a race.